LOVED YOU Always

NATALINA REIS

© 2016 *Loved You Always* by Natalina Reis

Loved You Always is a work of fiction. All names, characters, events and places found therein are either from the author's imagination or used fictitiously. Any similarity to persons alive or dead, actual events, locations, or organizations is entirely coincidental and not intended by the author.

For information, contact the publisher, Hot Tree Publishing.

WWW.HOTTREEPUBLISHING.COM

Editing: Hot Tree Editing

Cover Designer: Claire Smith

Interior Design: RMGraphx

ISBN-10: 1-925448-50-9

ISBN-13: 978-1-925448-50-4

10 9 8 7 6 5 4 3 2 1

Dedication

To my sister, Marilia, who is and always will be my best friend.

Chapter One

Friends Forever

Together forever; that was our motto. Jeremy and me, best friends forever. Come hell or high water, nothing would ever separate us. We met in preschool when my parents moved to Jem's neighborhood, and we weathered elementary, secondary, and even college together. We completed each other; Jem with his blond, curly hair, me with my pale skin and straight hair. His six feet two, my five four; his love for fast food, my love for everything gourmet. We were as different as humanly possible, and maybe because of that we fit together like two halves of a whole.

Throughout our childhood and early teen years we had shared everything; every thought, every feeling, every doubt. It felt right to share our most intimate selves with each other and, at some point, we were completing each other's sentences. At thirteen, Jem confided in me when Janet, the neighborhood beauty, bestowed upon him his first kiss. Soon after, I returned the confidence by telling him about my "lip encounter" with Steve, the school jock. When he got to second base with Alice, Jem ran home to call and tell me all about it, and when Sam accidentally touched my breast during a movie, I almost skipped the end of the feature to call Jem. Jem's shoulders had always been there for a good cry and vice versa. We were so close that people in our families began calling us the Siamese twins, Jem and Em. Even our names rhymed.

All of that changed—at least for me—when we were about sixteen. That summer, Jem went on vacation abroad with his parents; I stayed behind and worked all summer at a local pharmacy, saving money for college. Upon his return, Jem had a suitcase full of stories to tell me, as usual. Camping out in my room that weekend, we settled to share our summers like we had always done before. However, as Jem recounted his whirlwind romance with a pretty, young French girl, my feelings about sharing radically changed. This was different; this did not make me feel like I was a part of it. This hurt, and made me feel left out and lonely.

I didn't want him to share the details of his sexual encounters with this foreigner; neither did I want to hear about how sad he was to leave her behind. I wanted to hear how he had missed me and how he had been unable to enjoy himself without me. I felt guilty for that, and then angry at myself. By the time it was my turn to share an account of my summer I had decided I was not willing to share certain things anymore, so I shared innocuous events without ever touching on serious feelings. I needed time to get used to this new twist in our relationship.

It took me a few weeks to fully realize I was in love with my best friend.

Here we were now in college, in our habitual scene, lying on our backs across my bed, my legs stretched out along the wall, his curly hair on my belly. We had done this a million times throughout our lives, but it sure felt different now, in this unseasonable hot autumn day. His hair tickled my exposed midsection, and I wrapped my fingers around his silky curls as he told me about this girl he had been seeing, Lisa. I did not want to hear about his woes with this idiotic girl who did not value him as she should. I certainly did not want to know how much he cared for her and how much he was hurting. My fingers yearned to burrow into his hair in earnest. My left hand, lying between us, ached to slide over his tanned shoulder and caress his naked chest. This was torture, and I did not know what to do about it.

"She doesn't get me like you do," Jem was saying as I tried to focus on his words and forget about the tingles coursing through my whole body.

"Why don't you dump her?" The suggestion slipped through my lips before I could stop it. First rule of our relationship: never ever suggest an action unless solicited by the other party. "Sorry. I didn't mean to say that out loud."

I heard Jem chuckle a little. Then he wiggled onto his left side, head now turned directly toward me. "Where did that come from, Em?"

Oh, God! The movement of his head pulled my shirt higher. I now could feel the heat of his skin on my own, and my heart took off at a gallop. "It's just... well, she doesn't seem right for you, that's all," I said, feebly trying to control my own heartbeat.

"What's wrong?" he asked suddenly. "Your heart is going crazy." Of course he could hear it. His ear was almost centered on my chest.

"I don't know what you're talking about," I protested, willing myself to calm down.

His right hand came up and the next thing I know, he had his warm palm spread across my heart. "Wow, it's even worse now," he said. *Of course it is, you fool. You have your hand on my breast.*

Propping himself up on his elbows, Jem rolled onto his belly and stared at me with those gorgeous blue eyes of his. I felt my heart swell like a marshmallow over a fire and, at that moment, I hated him as much as I loved him. How do you tell your best friend in the world—someone who sees you as an asexual being—that you are so in love with him it hurts?

"Are you sure you're okay?" he asked again. "You've been acting a little weird lately." That was the understatement of the year. I was in a permanent state of semipanic when I was around him. On one hand I didn't want to let him go, to put some much-needed distance between us or at least establish some boundaries. On the other hand, my body burned at the mere sight of him, and I was so scared that one of these days I was going to do something I would regret forever. I did not want to lose my best friend.

"I'm fine," I promised. "Just a little tired."

He rolled himself on his back again, this time alongside my body. His was warm, and the spots where our bodies actually touched felt scorched and achy. I bit my tongue hard, drawing blood. "Let's take a nap, then," he said with infuriating calm.

After a few minutes, I chanced a quick glance at him. He had closed his eyes, and his chest was moving rhythmically to the sound of his quiet breathing. He had fallen asleep. *The sleep of the innocent.* No such luck for me. I watched him sleep for a little while. So handsome, so sweet....

Slowly, I propped myself on my elbow and my hand moved as if of its own accord to rest across his chest. Oh crap! What was I doing? But his skin was so smooth, so warm.... Throwing caution to the wind, I allowed my hand to explore his muscled chest in gentle, circular caresses. Jem was a heavy sleeper. He had been known to walk in his sleep, much to my amusement. This wouldn't wake him.

My brain had stopped functioning at a rational level, and my instincts were quickly taking over. He moaned a little, startling me for a second. Emboldened by his moan of pleasure, I slid my hand lower, toward his exposed belly muscles. He moaned again. I should have stopped, but the fire in my body was burning hot and I had relinquished all control, it seemed.

This can't be me, I thought as I lowered my face toward his. My parched lips found his forehead first, then the bridge of his nose, the corner of his mouth. He was still moaning gently and I wanted to believe I was the reason. I covered his lips with mine and, to my great surprise, he responded. His lips opened up to mine, and what had started with timid exploration turned into an explosion of passion. His arms encased me in a warm embrace and pulled me fully on top of him.

"I have waited so long for this," he whispered.

I couldn't believe my ears. Was it true? He really felt about me the same way I felt about him? My heart was so full I thought it would explode. I straddled him and turned to liquid as I realized he was reacting to me in a way I'd never thought possible. His eyes were still closed when I supported myself on his chest, palms spread out, half afraid I was dreaming. His hips moved slowly underneath me, and it was my turn to moan.

I had to feel his lips again. I leaned over and kissed him. Holy crap! He was such a good kisser. I melted even further. "I love you, Jem," I whispered over his mouth. "I have always loved you."

"I love you, too," he whispered into my lips. "I love you so much, Lisa."

Chapter Two

The Return

The phone buzzed again and I frowned as my students' heads snapped up at the sound. That's just what they needed, another distraction.

"Keep writing, children. It's only my phone. Ignore it."

Of course, they wouldn't be so interested in the sound if I hadn't stupidly picked the annoying robot beeps of R2-D2 as my ringtone and forgotten to put the phone on silent as I always did. Who would be calling me at this hour anyway? My boyfriend would never call me in school and everyone else knew I couldn't get to the phone most of the day, and that if it was something urgent texting was the way to go. I was curious. The phone had rung three times in a row already.

"Ms. Lambert, why don't you pick it up and check who it is?" You can't fault a ten-year-old's logic. Teachers were not supposed to answer their cell phones during the instructional day, but I smiled sweetly and decided that if the phone rang again, I would pick it up and give whoever was calling me at such an inconvenient time a piece of my mind.

"Class, you have another five minutes or so to finish your writing assignment," I said, meandering through the classroom and realizing a lot of the students had not made much progress. "This counts as two grades, guys. Put in your best effort."

Writing was not their forte or even something they remotely enjoyed doing. Every time I mentioned the word write—even if it was to tell them to write their names—I was met with a flood of moans and groans. For someone like me, who loved the written word, this seriously rankled.

Just as I approached the opposite end of the classroom, my phone beeped frantically again. That time, I rushed to my desk, dodging moving chairs and stretched-out feet, and with a flourish I snapped the cell phone up to my ear.

"Who's this?" Annoyance was obvious in my voice. I really hated being called during class.

On the other end there was a lot of background noise, music playing loudly and lots of people talking. "Em? Is that you?" The voice sounded strangely familiar, but the noise around it muffled it.

"Yes, it's Emily Lambert." Now I was really pissed off. "Who's this?"

"It's me, Jem."

I held on to the sides of my desk for fear of falling. Jem?

In my surprise I must have been quiet for a tad too long, because he spoke again. "Are you still there, Em? Hello?"

"Jem? Where are you?" Almost five years since I'd seen

him or talked to him, and that's what I come up with?

"At the airport. JFK." That would explain all the noise. "Waiting for my connector flight."

I was almost afraid to ask. "Are you coming home?" I squeezed my eyes shut, but opened them again when one of my students giggled. I placed a finger in front of my lips to quiet him down.

"Yes. I will be in town in a few hours." His voice still didn't seem familiar to me, distorted by all the noise in the background. "I'm staying at the Fairfield by the mall. Can we have dinner together?"

I surveyed my classroom and noticed several kids snickering. They undoubtedly thought I was talking to a boyfriend. Fifth graders were notorious for being matchmakers. "Listen, Jem. I'm in class right now and can't talk. Call me back when you land here."

"Sorry. My internal clock is still on European time." A loudspeaker muffled his next words. "—missed you, Em. I'll call you back in a few hours."

I was rooted to the tiled floor. Had I suffered a stroke of sorts and dreamed the whole exchange? Jem, who had hightailed to Europe almost five years ago without so much as a good-bye, had just called me and asked me to dinner? What did that mean? Or did it mean anything at all?

"Ms. Lambert, it's almost time for dismissal." The little red-haired girl was almost apologetic for interrupting my spaced-out state. Her voice brought me back to earth.

"Sorry, kiddos. A surprising call, that's all." A few of them stole glances at each other. "Let's put your writing journals away and pack your bags."

For the next hour, I almost forgot the unexpected call and focused on the job of dismissing a whole class of excited fifth graders and planning my lessons for the next day.

My drive home left me too much time to dwell on what had happened though. What could he possibly want with me? When he left, literally overnight, he had also broken my heart into a million pieces. He may not have been aware of my feelings for him, but he knew we had been best friends since childhood. How could he just up and leave without saying anything at all? For the past few years there had been no calls, no messages, not even a Facebook post or a Tweet. It was like he was purposely avoiding any contact. I knew he was in Europe because his mom, blissfully unaware of our falling out, kept me up with his comings and goings—what little she herself knew about his life away from home.

What had possibly possessed him to leave everything and everyone he knew and loved just like that? In my head, I had come up with all kinds of crazy scenarios. Deep down, I wanted him to have a great reason for what he did; I wanted to have a reason to forgive him. But no matter what I came up with, nothing seemed to justify his actions enough. In the end, I concluded that my best friend had followed some skirt— as he was known to do from time to time—and forsaken all others.

By the time I parked my car in the garage, I was fuming. All the anger I had felt all those years ago had been regurgitated tenfold. How dare he stay away for this long, only to show up all of a sudden and ask me to dinner? And why was he not staying with his parents in Florida? Was he hiding from them, too?

Heavy bag in tow, I walked up the stairs to my condo, stopping only to check my mailbox. Earlier that day I had planned to have an easy night—a cup of hot coffee in my pajamas, a book, and maybe a romantic movie before turning in. My boyfriend, Dave, was out of town and I had no wish to do anything that involved leaving the house. Now I was facing an awkward evening with the man who was once my best friend, the man I had fiercely loved for so long. What did he want after all this time? And why was my heart doing a little step dance inside my chest?

Instead of changing into my comfortable clothes like I normally did, I refreshed my hair and makeup. My eyes, narrowed to slits, looked at my reflection without actually seeing it. In my mind, I was painting a picture of Jem as I'd seen him that last time, before I knew it was indeed the last time. His handsome, boyish face framed by a mass of blond, untamed curls had seemed a little withdrawn, sad even. I remembered asking him what was wrong and the shrug he had given me in response.

We'd watched a movie that night, *Say Anything*, one of our favorites. Arguing about what John Cusack should or should not have done in the story was a longtime favorite activity for the two of us. I always thought he should have told her where to stick that pen of hers, and Jem insisted that she just needed to be reminded of how much she loved him. In the end, we both agreed it had to be one of the most romantic movies ever. After the movie, we had stayed up until the wee hours of the morning, talking quietly so we wouldn't disturb my sleeping parents. I was still living at home then, saving to get my own place. Jem had long left the nest, but his roommates were loud and nosy, so we spent most of our time at my parents' house instead.

"What's wrong with you tonight?" I asked at one point, noticing the long silences and the wistful looks he kept throwing my way.

"Nothing." He was lying. I could always tell when he was lying; his eyes rolled a little upward, avoiding mine. "I just want to remember this moment."

I had smacked him across an arm playfully. "Stop being mushy. It makes me feel weird." It made me feel hot inside and ready to do something I would possibly regret later.

The next day he was gone. His mom and dad seemed to be at as much of a loss as I was.

"He left most of his things behind, his roommates told us. Took only one suitcase and some money he had saved. Left us a note saying he would be gone for a while, but not to worry because everything was okay."

Shortly after that, his mother informed me she had received news from the runaway son. He was fine. He was in Europe with a girl he fell in love with. My heart broke into a million pieces and, being honest, it was still in pieces even after five years.

The phone buzzed. How long had I been staring at myself in the mirror? My hands, gripping the marble counter for dear life, had gone numb and my throat was dry. The phone kept ringing even as I snatched it from the counter. It was an unknown number. I knew I should probably ignore the call, but the goody-two-shoes in me couldn't make herself do it.

"Hello?"

"Em, it's me, Jem." As if I wouldn't recognize his voice. It had been a long time, but his voice was engraved in my memory forever. My best friend. My love. "Can we meet for dinner?"

I found that I had lost the ability to think or articulate thoughts rationally. "Where?" I had become monosyllabic.

"Is our old hangout still open?" The Old Bookstore. Yes, it was still open. "Can we meet there in twenty minutes?"

Not knowing what to wear for such an occasion, I slipped into a pair of jeans and a comfortable T-shirt. Why should I dress up for him? I was almost at the door when I made a full turn and went to change. I didn't want him to think I had let myself go in his absence. God knew he didn't need more air pumped into his already inflated ego. From the inside of my closet I dug up a sexy midnight-blue top. As a compromise, I kept my comfortable jeans on.

A bundle of nerves had settled in my stomach. I was going to throw up at any moment. *Damn it, Jem!* Even after all this time I still felt like a teenager when it came to him. I was twenty-nine, but my heart didn't seem to be aware of that.

Good thing there was little traffic, because I wasn't sure how I got to the restaurant. My head was so full I must have driven on autopilot. The next thing I knew I was parking in the tiny parking lot, my hands slipping off the steering wheel and my heart on a drumming rampage.

The Old Bookstore, in spite of its name, did not sell books.

It was a coffee shop that had been built in an old bookstore. Leftover bookshelves lined the walls, packed with books and caffeine paraphernalia. Small wooden tables and chairs peppered the old floors, and overstuffed armchairs in every corner invited patrons to read over a cup of steamy coffee.

My heart jumped to my throat when I saw him. Alone in one of our favorite booths, beautiful and youthful as always. *Will he ever grow old?* His blond hair was tousled around his boy-next-door face, a faded strip of freckles across the bridge of his nose setting the stage for his amazing blue eyes. For a moment I contemplated a quick getaway, but his eyes met mine before I could do it. A smile curved his generous lips and he waved.

With a big dry gulp, I forced myself to walk toward the booth, but I couldn't muster more than a grimace. As much as I loved that beautiful jerk, I was too angry at him to offer him the comfort of a forgiving smile.

Standing, Jem came toward me with his arms open wide and, before I could stop him, I found myself enfolded in his embrace, crushed against his chest and with his lips on my face. "Oh my God, Emily Rose, I missed you so much. You are a sight for sore eyes."

How dare he kiss me like nothing had happened? But I couldn't extricate myself from his embrace. It was so good. It felt like home in his long, warm arms, the subtle scent of him intoxicating me all over again. My arms were itching to reciprocate the hug, but I was paralyzed and they remained solidly along my sides. He didn't seem to notice and continued to squeeze me against him, depositing kiss after kiss on my flushed cheeks and nose.

Finally, he pulled me away from him a little and scanned my body from top to bottom. "You look as gorgeous as ever," he exclaimed. He sounded so sincere my heart thawed just a little. "I can't believe I'm here with you. At last."

Still silent, my lips glued together in shock and fear of what may come out of them, I sat across from him in the booth. My breathing was erratic and my hands were still sweaty. I wiped them on my pants and swallowed again.

"You look like you're in shock." Really? And he was surprised? "I have so much to tell you."

Amazed at how casual he sounded after such a long absence, I snapped. "What the hell, Jem! You were gone—without as much as a good-bye—for five freaking years and you expect me to just pick up where we left off?" It came out much louder than I intended and I noticed a few of the other patrons staring at us. I lowered my voice. "You've got some nerve."

Jem's face had fallen a bit. He'd truly thought I was going to welcome him with open arms and forget the fact that I hadn't heard from him in all this time. Was he really that arrogant?

"I know. You have every right to be mad."

Hell yes, I had the right to be raving mad. Afraid that I might actually breathe fire, I lowered my eyes to my lap.

"I was an idiot to leave without saying good-bye. I didn't think I could handle it." *He* couldn't handle it? But he could handle leaving his best friend with no warning? "It was so hard for me to leave, but—"

"But what, Jem? What?" I exploded, all the anger of

the past years flowing through me and out my mouth. "It's not hard. 'Hey, Em, I'll be moving to another country and probably won't see you for a few years. I'll write or Skype you sometime.' See? Not hard at all."

Jem's face had turned a mottled shade of red. At least he still had the good sense to be embarrassed. "I had a good reason, Em. I really did." His gorgeous sapphire eyes were pleading. In the past that would have been enough to mollify me, but a lot had happened since then and I was not going to allow him to appease me that easily.

"What could have possibly been the reason to abandon everything, run to a foreign country, and have no contact with your best friend? At all!" Fury colored my words, which came out fast and sharp. "Tell me! Can you tell me?"

He lowered his eyes to his lap. "I can't. Not yet."

What kind of explanation was that? Did he really expect me to trust him like I used to? Trust was one of the casualties of his actions.

"Jeremy Peter," I said, knowing all too well he absolutely hated his full name. When we were kids he made me promise never ever to call him that. Well, it was my turn to break a promise. "You can't even come up with one good reason for your choices. Why did you even call me? Why did you come back?"

His voice was a whisper. "I miss you, Emily Rose. I miss you so much."

I swung my legs to the side and slid out of the booth. "You didn't miss me enough to let me know you were alive." The miserable look in his eyes gave me pause. For a fraction of a second. The anger burning in my heart was too hot, too strong. I lashed out. "Don't call me again. You're dead to me, Jeremy Peter. Dead." And I walked out of the coffee shop, a bitter taste in my mouth and tears burning in my eyes.

How dare he come back to my life just as I was finally getting used to the idea of a life without him? Just as my heart was healing? I had a loving, stable man in my life now. One I could count on being there for me no matter what.

I drove like a maniac all the way home and threw myself on my bed, clothes and all, for a good cry. Hating myself for shedding tears over Jem again, I punched the pillows and kicked the blankets off the bed. It didn't satisfy me. Using the pillow as a muffler, I screamed as loud and for as long as I could, only stopping when a deep burning crawled up my throat.

"I hate you, Jem. I hate you." All the energy produced by my anger ebbing away, I wiped my eyes with the back of my hands and sighed, feeling childish and stupid. "God, I hate that I don't hate you. I love you. I will always love you."

Chapter Three

Old Friends and Witches

With dozens of pictures scattered on the floor around me, I pined over one particular photo. I don't know how long I stared at it before the sound of someone approaching woke me up from my daze. "What do you got there?"

My head snapped up to the tall, dark man standing a few inches from me. "Dave, you scared me." Because I had gone to another time and another place. I handed him the picture with a little sigh. "How did you get in?"

"You left the door unlocked." Crap! I couldn't keep my head out of the clouds. "Wow! You look totally different in this picture," he exclaimed, sitting down on the edge of the couch. "What's with the hair?"

I laughed at his surprise. "I went through a stage. I wanted to embrace my Asian ancestry fully." I giggled again, realizing how silly that sounded now. "I got a bob and bangs and wore kimono-cut dresses for almost a whole year."

Dave stared at me, his mouth slightly open. "You're not even fully Asian," he sputtered. "I mean, you look cute but—it's not you."

My dad was a military man, a hard-core marine with a heart of gold. He had met my mom in Japan during one of his assignments and—as the story went—fell in love and got married. My mom was fluent in English, working for the American consulate in Tokyo, so the fact that my father could barely say thank you in Japanese had not been an obstacle to their romance. Unlike my sister, who favored my dad in everything but his height, I was all Japanese. My eyes were slightly less slanted than my mom's, but everything else was as ethnic as you can get without actually putting on a regional costume and speaking in Japanese. Sick of being compared to my blonde, round-eyed sister, I decided to totally embrace my Japanese heritage. That's when the picture Dave held in his hand had been taken.

"I like you better the way you are right now," he declared, handing the picture back to me. He went down on his knees, gingerly avoiding the pictures on the floor, and kissed me. "I love your beautiful, long black hair and your amazing black eyes." He swept a hand over my hair as if to prove his point. "And I adore those red, full lips."

Lost in the kiss, my mind wandered to another time when someone else had told me pretty much the same thing—minus the kiss. I remembered Jem saying those same words when I admitted to him I hated the way I looked. I so wanted to be like my sister. *Pull yourself together, woman.* Here I was, kissing my boyfriend with my mind on another guy.

Dave pulled our lips apart and I opened my eyes, a little dazed. "So, should we stay in or go out for a bite?" He was always hungry. That big ex-marine body of his seemed to digest food as if it were water. I laughed and began collecting the photographs from the floor. "Joe's Shack? I could go for a giant burger and fries."

"Sure. Let me pick up this mess." Dave joined me as I stored the pictures in my over-the-top romantic box. When I looked up, he was staring at another picture, squinting in concentration. "What?"

"Who's this? You guys look pretty chummy." I picked the photo from his hand, and my heart clenched. It was a picture of Jem and me a few days before he left. We looked young and happy, his arm draped over my shoulders and a big smile on his handsome face. I, on the other hand, had my face turned up to his, a look of utter devotion in my eyes. I was so obviously in love with him it was embarrassing.

I threw the picture in the box with the others. "Just a friend." As if.

"I've never met him." Dave could be very obtuse when he chose to.

Keeping my eyes on the work at hand and far away from his, I answered in what I hoped was a dismissive tone, "A childhood friend. He lived next door for most of my life."

"Where is he now?" *God, Dave! Will you just let it go?*

"He left five years ago, but he just came back to town." I so did not want to talk about this with him. "We are not friends anymore."

From the corner of my eye I noticed the look of disbelief

in his hazel eyes. "What happened?"

Giving up on the pretense, I raised my eyes to his and shook my head. "Dave, I don't want to talk about it. He was my best friend and he left years ago without so much as a good-bye. He called me when he came back to town, and I don't even want to think about him. It makes me mad." My voice had risen in a crescendo of anger, I realized. I *was* very angry at Jem, even after all these years.

Dave threw his hands up in the air. "Sorry. I won't ask again." He pulled me into his arms and kissed the top of my head. "Come on. Nothing a greasy burger can't fix." I had to laugh. Men and their stomachs!

Eating out with Dave was always fun. The man had an inexhaustible hunger for new foods. The weirder the better. I loved that about him. I was myself a foodie who enjoyed trying new dishes as often as possible. I had dated guys before who were so picky and limited in terms of their taste buds that we invariably ended up eating at hamburger or Italian places. Nothing against Italian cuisine—which I loved, by the way—but my stomach craved the kind of variety those more traditional restaurants could not offer me.

That night we had settled on a little Belgian bistro a few miles from the house. My taste buds were dancing in anticipation of the amazing *frites* they served. I didn't often eat fried food, but french fries were an obsession of mine. Dave knew that and, seeing my gloomy mood, steered me to the Petit Chef.

"Do you think the chef here is really small?" Dave asked, pulling the chair out for me. He was a gentleman with impeccable manners most of the time.

I giggled. "Never saw him, but judging by the restaurant's name that's a very strong possibility. Maybe we should ask."

When the young waitress came to take our orders, Dave didn't hesitate. "Tell me"—he squinted, trying to read her name tag—"Jordan, is the chef really small like the name of this place implies?"

The girl looked confused. "The name?" Hell, she didn't even know what the name of her workplace meant in English. Wasn't she just a little curious?

"Never mind." Dave gave up, stealing a disbelieving glance at me. "Bring us a beer and a Coke." I had never been much of a drinker.

We had a lovely dinner of *frites* and mussels, shared a giant Belgian waffle topped with a mountain of whipped cream, and espresso. By the time Dave dropped me off at my place I was feeling better. We said good night with one of Dave's long, sexy kisses at the door, and I watched him get in his car and leave. He was a good man: handsome, smart, and fun to be around. I was a lucky woman.

A book in hand, I cuddled under my bedcovers for a quick read before going to sleep. Tomorrow my young students expected me to be just plain Ms. Lambert, alert and ready for a long day of learning. My eyelids were getting heavy, and my thoughts were beginning to drift when I heard the phone ring. Damn! Forgot to silence it again. I reached out for it and almost dropped it when I saw the name on the caller ID.

"What do you want?" I yelled. "It's almost midnight."

Jem's voice caressed my ears, and I hated him for the way

he could still make me feel. "Sorry, Em. I really need to talk to you. Can I come over? I want to explain—"

"Go to hell, Jem. What is there to say that you couldn't have a few years ago?"

"Please, Emily Rose, let me explain." His voice, low and pleading, was wearing down my resolve. "I don't want you to hate me."

That was the real problem; I didn't hate him. Even after all this time, I still loved him. "I'm outside. Can I come in?"

Hating myself for it, I jumped out of bed and, forgetting I was in my pajamas, sprinted to the door to let him in. There he was in all his male glory, jeans low on his hips, a tight black T-shirt that revealed well-sculpted muscles, and a short black jacket in sharp contrast with his dirty-blond hair. When he raised his ocean-blue eyes to me, I swooned. For a moment I forgot he had left me, that he'd kept me guessing for five years; I forgot I had an amazing boyfriend who loved me and whom I adored. Jem still had the magic power to turn me into an idiot with just one look.

He walked past me, looking appropriately contrite.

"You better make it quick. Some of us work for a living." I hoped I sounded convincingly irate.

We sat across from each other in the living room, ill at ease and silent. I felt a ridiculous urge to offer him something to drink, but quickly dismissed it. Five years and he still felt so familiar, as if he had never left.

"Nice place, Em." His voice surprised me out of my stupor. "Have you lived here long?"

I was not up to chitchat. The longer he stayed, the more

blurred the lines between reality and my wishful thinking would become. "You said you wanted to explain yourself."

Jem cleared his throat and brushed his fingers through his unruly curls. "I didn't leave you because I wanted to. Not exactly." I waited patiently to hear what he would come up with to justify what he had done. "Remember Tina?" How could I forget? She had been the girl he was dating right before his vanishing act. I never liked any of the myriad of girls he paraded by me throughout the years. In his defense, he was always convinced he was truly in love with these girls, but the relationships never lasted long.

I nodded.

"Well, something happened. She witnessed a murder and became a target herself. I couldn't leave her at a time like that."

Confused, I shook my head. "I don't understand. What do you mean, you couldn't leave her like that?"

"She was in danger. Mortal danger." I was still not understanding how all this had anything to do with him. "She had two choices. Stay and be killed or flee. She decided to go out of the country, away from her family and everything she had ever known. Alone. I had to do something. So I volunteered to go with her."

The words made sense, but nothing else did. "You *volunteered* to go with her? You barely knew her." The bitterness in my voice surprised me enough to shut me up.

"I made a mistake, Emily Rose. I thought I was in love with her and…." His voice trailed off.

I looked at him, eyes burning with the threat of angry tears.

Having him here was almost like old times, except it wasn't. The times he had spent at my place, hanging out for hours on end, had been happy times. Having him here in my living room now was not. Did he really believe I was going to accept his half-assed explanation? "You want me to believe that crap? That you left your family and best friend to keep a girlfriend company? A girl you had known for maybe two months? Couldn't you come up with a more plausible explanation?"

In his defense, he looked utterly miserable and uncomfortable. "I was afraid you wouldn't believe me, but it's true. All of it. Every second of the whole miserable, stupid thing." His head dropped to his chest as he brought his hands up to rub the back of his neck. "I was so freaking stupid, Em. I guess I've never been too smart when it comes to women, but I really messed up with this one."

Oh my God! Was he really going to do the whole my-heart-broke act? And why was I leaning forward in wordless invitation for further details? "Yes, you messed up royally, Jem. I'm not sure I'll ever be able to forgive you." *You broke my heart, you fool.* I wouldn't say it out loud, but it was true nevertheless. He broke it every time he "fell in love." The difference with this one was that he had also abandoned me.

"I know. I hate myself for it. I knew it was a mistake the minute I landed in Europe." He was talking to the floor, as if afraid to look me in the eye.

I doubted I looked very friendly at that moment. My face burned with the anger I felt in my heart. "And it took you five years to come back?"

His intense blue eyes locked on to mine finally. "I couldn't leave. If I left, they would trace me back to where she was, find her and most likely kill her. I couldn't do that to her. I had to see it through."

I bit my tongue and tasted blood. "So what changed now that you could finally leave?" Jem licked his lips, and in a nanosecond I was taken back to that afternoon in my room when I lost all common sense and had kissed him while he slept. I squeezed my hands together, trying to control the sudden tremors. "What changed?" My voice sounded raw and strangely quiet.

"Tina got tired of living in France and agreed to move elsewhere," he explained, wiping his hands along his thighs. "It was my chance to bail."

Silence fell and wrapped itself around us with the tightness and roughness of a taut rope, squeezing and pulling with each second that passed. I couldn't decide whether to hug or slap him as he sat facing me, looking like a puppy begging for mercy. *Shit, Jeremy Peter! What am I going to do about you?*

"Please, say you forgive me," he whispered, breaking the oppressive silence in the room. "I missed my best friend. There was not a single day in the last five years that I didn't think of you. You have no idea how many times I caught myself dialing your number. I know I don't deserve it, but I want back into your life, Emily Rose." In a swift move, he sprang out of his seat and dropped to the floor on his knees right before me. Before I could react, he had taken hold of my hands. "I missed you."

My chest felt tight, as if an elephant had sat on it. I suddenly yearned to run and hide in a dark room. I stared down at the ground, afraid of what may come out of my mouth should I choose to open it—not much danger of that happening, considering my lips were glued together tightly. Hyperventilating slightly, I shifted in my seat and pulled my hands from his. It was all moving too fast for me. Too much information and too many emotions swirled around together in a tornado of confusion and anxiety.

Jem sat back on the rug and wrapped his long arms around his knees. "I get it." His voice was quiet and submissive, and my heart flipped again. "I really do. You need time to think it all over. I'm moving into my parents' house in a couple days." He stood and hesitated for a moment. "I…. Good night, Em, and thank you for listening to me."

Time passed, but I remained frozen in that spot. I'm not sure how long I sat there after he left, but the next morning I walked around school like a zombie, half from lack of sleep, the other half from confusion and mixed-up feelings. What was I going to do? Should I forgive him and go back to the close relationship we had before he left? Or should I let it go? Do the Band-Aid thing and just pull it off once and for all?

So many questions, and no answers.

***

"You're kidding me!" The exclamation exploded out of Celia so loudly everybody in the coffee shop turned their eyes toward us. She waved them off absentmindedly and lowered her voice just a smidgen. "He's back and came to apologize?"

Scanning the room for familiar faces, I let out a sigh of relief when I couldn't find any. "Yes, he came to my house after midnight to apologize."

Celia brought her hand to her lips. "Hell has frozen over. What did you say?" Her big round eyes opened wide as she checked for a reaction in mine. "Shit! You didn't say you'd forgive him, did you? He made you suffer for five long years. He must pay for it."

I shifted uncomfortably on my seat. "I'm not sure he hasn't already," I said feebly, my mind searching for the right words. "I don't think his life has been that great either."

My sister planted her hands on her hips with a flourish. "Hell no, sis! You are not doing this to yourself again. I'm sure his life in France was totally miserable because, you know, who has fun in France ever?" Sarcasm dripped from her mouth and out of her blue eyes. I had told her he had been in France—with Tina.

"He wanted to come back and couldn't," I continued. Who was I trying to convince? My sister or myself? "It's in the past, and I have a great boyfriend and a good life and—"

My hand was cocooned in hers. "And what? I know that in your heart of hearts you have not forgotten him. Not completely. You need to be tough this time. Tell him to go find another Tina and go f—"

I stuck a finger over her lips, preventing her from cursing out loud. I abhorred cursing. The teacher in me cringed anytime my ears were assailed by bad language. Jem had always made fun of me because of it. He said I was an old woman trapped in the body of a young one. I didn't mind. I loved it when he teased me.

"I know, I know. Don't worry about it. I have moved on."

I sounded a lot more certain than I really felt. "He is the past. Dave is the future."

My sister squeezed my hand. "He was not even the past, honey. He never loved you. Not that way." I knew that, but it still stung. A lot. I felt tears burning in the back of my eyes, and a wave of heat climbed up my neck to my face. "Come on, let's go and exorcise that son of a bitch from your life."

My sister was a true believer in rituals and magic. She claimed that even though I didn't believe magic existed—not the hocus-pocus kind—the simple act of performing a ritual of some kind to exorcise bad vibes would make me feel better. She had ceremonies for everything. When we were in high school, she made me write this long letter to a friend who had betrayed me and then dragged me to a clearing in the woods by the school and burned it with great aplomb. She was known for muttering gibberish she called spells, and you could always find a myriad of crystals inside her pockets.

"Oh God, what are you going to make me do this time?" My horrified tone made her laugh. A few seconds later she was sprinting down the street, dragging me behind her. "Where are we going, crazy woman?"

"To Polka Dots & Eye of Newt. I know the owner, a witch." Celia was always able to say the most ridiculous things and sound totally reasonable. "She'll have a good spell to get that asshole out of your life for good." Deep inside I wanted to yell, *He's not an asshole*, but I knew she was right. He had left me, his best friend from childhood, to follow a stupid girl he barely knew.

Polka Dots & Eye of Newt was a quaint little shop with a

black canopy over the front door and a bay window promising the onlooker a collection of oddities and curiosities should they decide to enter. I sighed loudly. "Celia, this is ridiculous. How is magic going to help me?"

I was unceremoniously pulled through the doorway and into the dim store. The air was heavy with exotic smells and I felt an irresistible urge to sneeze and scratch my nose. I noticed a tiny, skinny young woman standing behind the counter. Her huge square glasses had slid down her nose and were now precariously hanging from the upturned tip.

"Marcy," my sister called. That sounded like a ludicrous name for a witch. "This is my sister, Emily Rose. She needs a spell or potion to get this guy to stay out of her life for good."

Marcy, the so-called witch, looked up at us and smiled. She was missing a tooth in front, and her face was covered in freckles. "Hey, Celia. Pleasure to meet you, Emily Rose. Boyfriend trouble?"

"No, no boyfriend trouble at all." I hurried to correct her before she put some kind of spell on poor Dave. "And it's Em."

"Someone from her past," Celia clarified. "Can you help her?"

The witch, her bright red hair wrapped tightly into a bun on the top of her head, smiled a big semitoothless smile and waved her hand toward the counter. "Come closer. Of course I have something to do the trick."

I couldn't help it. "Why the toothless look?" I thought maybe she wanted to look more like a real witch.

Her smile was contagious, and I found that I actually liked

this little witch. "I fell riding my bike and busted a tooth a couple days ago. I'm waiting for my dentist to perform his magic." She giggled at the pun.

Part of me was disappointed. Without that tooth she looked like a cross between Pippi Longstocking and the Wicked Witch of the West. "Ouch. You're okay?"

"I'm fine. A little sore across the mouth, but it could have been a lot worse." Kudos for her positivity. I liked her. "So, you need to get rid of someone from your past. A boyfriend?"

She had led us into a small parlor and we were now sitting on two old but comfortable flowery couches. "No, just a very good friend."

"Who she loved more than life itself," my sister added with her usual dramatic flair. I gave her the look of death. It didn't faze her at all. "He's back after an absence of five years, during which he never called or wrote to her."

"That has to sting." Duh. It sure didn't feel *good*. "So we need to find something to keep this bastard at bay?"

"He came crawling back to her asking for forgiveness, and she'll give it to him, I'm sure." My sister, the seer. She had a point though. "You need to make her stop being such a pushover for this guy."

"I'm not a pushover." No one was listening to me. Marcy was chewing on the tip of one of her very long blue nails and scrunching her eyes as if in deep thought. I gave up and slid down into the cozy cushions.

"I need more information." Marcy's bright blue eyes were stuck on mine. "Why did he leave? And why is he back?"

We talked for a while, Pippi double-asking questions and

uttering hums as we answered. Finally satisfied, she sprang from her seat and ran to the back of the store. We could hear the sounds of glass hitting glass and the shuffling of papers. On her return, Marcy had a couple dust bunnies stuck to her hair and her orange sweater. "I got it!" The announcement was accompanied by her hand being thrust in front of me.

There was a small vial of a greenish liquid in her hand. "What's that?" If she thought I was going to drink that disgusting-looking concoction, she had another thing coming.

"It's a repellent potion." I almost fell off the couch. What? "You wear it like a perfume—it smells very nice—and it will keep him away from you. After a few weeks, he will be gone for good and will never bother you again."

She had to be kidding! My sister, knowing exactly what I was going to say, jumped in before I could open my mouth. "We'll take it. How much?"

"Free for friends." Because it wouldn't work. "Keep me apprised of what's happening. That's payment enough for me. Oh, and a cleansing couldn't hurt."

Was she suggesting I was dirty? "A cleansing?"

"Get some pictures of him, mementos of your past together, put them in a container and burn them. It will give you some closure." That actually sounded like a good idea. I had seen people do that in movies and I had always wanted to do it. Maybe this witch thing wouldn't be that bad after all.

"Thank you, Marcy." I walked toward the exit with my sister in tow. "It was very nice meeting you."

Back in the fresh air, I took a deep breath and looked at my crazy sister. Celia's beautiful, curly blonde hair was twirling around her head and face as the wind gusted all around us. I loved her dearly, but she could be such a pain in the you-know-what. "Thank you so much for this exhilarating experience."

Instead of getting upset at my deeply sarcastic tone, she laughed. "You're very welcome." Oblivious, as usual. "Don't let her quirky looks deceive you. Marcy's stuff really works."

I gave her a skeptical look. "Did you see the color of that potion? Do you really think it's safe to wear?"

We walked slowly, fighting against the strong wind, the edges of our sweaters flapping around us like flags. "Yes, absolutely. You need to wear that. It will work, you'll see. But we have to go to your place and pick up some stuff to burn."

The idea of burning anything that held a memory for me was suddenly not something I looked forward to in spite of my earlier excitement. "Maybe we could just skip that step, Celia." Aware that I sounded a little whiny, I bit my lip. "I know you're trying to help, but I'm a little overwhelmed right now."

In her usual exuberant fashion, my sister threw her arms around me in a bear hug. "I know, sis. You'll be okay."

We spent the rest of the day shopping, the usual go-to female strategy to cure all evils. Normally shopping would not be my chosen therapy—I actually despised it—but in this instance it seemed just the thing the doctor ordered. My wallet was not happy at the end of the day, as I walked into my house dragging more bags than Santa on Christmas Eve. Celia had taken a cab home with just as many—or more.

My couch was calling, so I threw all the bags on the floor of my bedroom, changed quickly into some yoga pants and a comfy T-shirt, and slid myself along the inviting expanse that was my sofa. Sleep must have taken me because the next thing I knew there was a loud banging on my door. Half asleep, I crawled off the couch and went to look through the peephole. The sight of both Dave and Jem standing together outside my door confused me so much I froze. Was I having a bizarre dream?

The knocking resumed even louder. "Yes?" I risked in a shaky voice.

"It's me, Dave. Will you open this damn door already?" His familiar voice soothed my nerves, but he did not sound happy. For a while now I had been thinking about giving Dave a key to my house, but the little nagging voice inside me that always seemed so unsure of everything wouldn't let me. He must have been waiting outside for some time.

When I opened the door I held my breath for a moment. It had not been a dream; Jem was indeed standing right next to Dave on my welcome mat. "Jem? What are you doing here?" Then, realizing I had totally ignored my own boyfriend, I stepped forward and rose on my tiptoes to kiss Dave on the lips. "Hi, Dave. Sorry. I was asleep."

Dave had a rare scowl on his face as he stepped inside quickly followed by Jem. "Aren't you going to introduce us?" Dave nodded toward Jem.

My heart skipped a beat. Did I really have to? "Sorry. Dave, this is Jeremy Peter, an old childhood friend." *Who abandoned me five years ago.* "Jem, this is Dave, my boyfriend." Jem's subtle start at the word boyfriend gave me a measure of satisfaction. Did he think I was going to stay home waiting for him to come back and not have a life? Shit, we weren't even romantically involved. "Jem has been away in Europe for the past few years and just came back."

Dave visibly relaxed as he slid an arm over my shoulders. "Nice to meet you, then, Jeremy." He stretched a welcoming hand toward the other man.

Jem, looking a little unsettled, shook his hand. "Thank you. Nice to meet you, too. And it's Jem."

Dave offered him one of his amazing, generous smiles and waved toward the living room. "Come in, come in." A wave of anger ran through me. How dare he? This was my house, not his. *But he's your boyfriend, stupid.* Swallowing my unreasonable resentment, I led the way into my living room and offered Jem a seat.

"So, how did the two of you meet?" *Damn it, Dave!*

Jem sat down and looked at Dave with a question in his eyes. I could almost hear him thinking, *Is this guy for real?* "Well, we met in preschool and have been friends ever since."

"We were friends until he left for Europe. We haven't seen or talked to each other since." My voice was bitter, I knew. And the anger I felt in my heart was certainly blazing out of my eyes as I stared at him. He gulped. "The question is how come you were both at my door at the same time?"

Dave, sitting next to me, pulled me against his side and kissed my cheek. "I came to get you and go grab a bite to eat, and Jeremy—I mean, Jem here—showed up almost exactly at the same time."

Unusually quiet, Jem looked from Dave to me and back. "I just came to say hi." If that wasn't the weakest excuse ever, I didn't know what was.

Dave stood up, towering over me with that skyscraper body of his. "Well, why don't you come with us for a bite? Then you two will have a chance to catch up, and I'll get to know you a little better." That sounded peachy. *Awkward, meet totally awkward.*

I jumped in, desperate to end this weird situation. "I'm sure Jeremy Peter is busy. Looking for a job and whatnot."

Jem's lip trembled. "Actually, I have nothing to do today. I just came from a job interview and I'm free for the evening."

I hate you. Except, I didn't.

"That's settled. Go put on something presentable, sweetheart." Dave could be so clueless sometimes. My pointed glares didn't seem to hold any meaning for him at all. Jem would have got it. In fact, I could tell he knew exactly what I was thinking, for a tiny smile appeared on the corner of his mouth. The devil was having fun!

No point in fighting it. I did what Dave had asked me, and in no time I was sitting at the Thai restaurant around the corner with my boyfriend and the man I had so fiercely loved most of my life. Not weird at all.

Jem sat right across from me at the small square table, and Dave sat to my left. This was going to be a very long meal. When Dave was studying the menu, I threw some I-will-kill-you looks in Jem's direction, but he shrugged them off with an infuriating smile. That thick-skinned side of him used to make me laugh. Now it made me want to scream.

When the waitress came for our orders, Jem looked up from the menu. "I will have the massaman curry, and the lady will have the seafood Pad Thai." I froze. He still remembered what I always ordered in Thai restaurants. "That was always your favorite." His voice had softened, and so did my heart.

"Wow, you guys really know each other well." Hard to tell whether Dave was annoyed or truly impressed. "And you still remember even after all these years."

"You never forget a good friend," Jem offered with a smile as he handed the menu to the waitress. Dave placed his order, and we were left to our own devices.

Dave didn't waste any time. "So, Jem, how come you moved to Europe? Job offer?"

I didn't waste any time either. "He followed a girl he had met and volunteered to go and be her companion and protector. Isn't that so thoughtful of him?" The barbs in my voice could not have gone unnoticed. Jem flinched, his lips stretching tight.

"Is that true? Protect her from what?" Dave asked, unwrapping his napkin and placing it on his lap.

With a strained smile, Jem fidgeted in his seat. "Kind of. I did follow this girl I knew because she had witnessed a crime and was in danger. I guess that sounds really dumb, doesn't it?" He looked defeated, and I almost felt sorry for him. Almost.

"Of course not." Magnanimous Dave. "If you loved this girl, why not?"

Jem shifted again, his hands smoothing invisible creases on the tablecloth. "The thing is I really didn't love her." His voice was quiet.

My wonderful, ever-sympathetic boyfriend bounced his

gaze from Jem to me a few times, obviously at a loss for words. I came to his rescue. "So, why did you? Why leave your family behind to follow a woman you didn't love?"

Jem's amazing blue eyes came to rest on mine, anger darkening them to the blue of an evening sky. "I don't know, Em. I really don't know why. It seemed like the right thing to do at the time. I've always been dumb when it comes to girls. Maybe I was running away…. I don't know." The intensity of his tone surprised me. He was not one for angry outbursts. Forever the appeaser, Jem was always the one to calm me down in the middle of a fight. "I can't start to explain how sorry I am."

"Don't be so hard on yourself, dude," Dave said. "We all have done stupid stuff in the name of love… or lust. You dust yourself off and start again."

Jem managed a smile. "My friend Em won't forget it so soon, I'm afraid." No, I wouldn't. Probably never. "And of all people in the world I want to make amends with, she is number one on my list."

I didn't turn, but I could feel Dave's eyes on me. "Is that true? You won't forgive him?"

Trying to keep my cool, but with my chest beginning to burn, I took a deep breath before talking. "He abandoned me. We had been best friends since preschool, and he left and stayed away for five years without as much as an e-mail letting me know he was alive and well."

"Well, honey, he couldn't do it without putting the girl's life in danger, could he?" It was infuriating when Dave was more rational than me. Why was he defending my idiot ex-friend?

I swallowed back a nasty retort. "He could have told me what he was doing right before he left. Then at least I would've known he wasn't just ignoring me." I was babbling and I knew it. "Can we change the subject? I'm going to end up with indigestion."

As if on cue the food arrived, defusing a very uncomfortable conversation. Pad Thai was comfort food, kind of like mac and cheese or mashed potatoes. My knotted stomach thanked me for it. I was famished and had to pace myself eating it, for fear of attracting the attention of the other patrons. Unlike me, Jem barely touched his food, playing with the floating pieces of vegetables and staring intently at his plate.

When our jasmine tea arrived, Jem had had enough. He stood up, thanked Dave for dinner and his kindness, and then looked at me, unsure of what to do next. For a moment I thought he was going to kiss my cheek, but in the end he gave me an awkward wave and left, leaving some money on the table.

"You could give him a break." Dave looked me in the eye, his fingers interlaced by his chin. He had the most impeccable table manners. "The poor guy is obviously repentant."

I bristled at his words. "I don't care. He left me hanging for five years. Let him squirm a little." Not my usual philosophy. I felt ashamed of my behavior even as I spoke. "Let's not talk about him." I stretched an arm over the table and held his hand. "We're finally alone. Are you spending the night?"

"Are you inviting me?" His eyes twinkled with mischief. I had to laugh.

"I am. We've been so busy, and it's been a couple weeks now—"

Not letting me finish my thought, he leaned over and kissed me, long and deep. I relaxed into his kiss. Dave's lips were like a good glass of red wine, warm and soothing.

"So, Celia took me to see a witch today," I said when we came up for air.

"No way!"

Jem forgotten, we spent the rest of the evening together chatting and enjoying each other's company.

When we finally left, I was suddenly so exhausted I could barely keep my eyes open on our way home. Dave noticed and left me to sleep it off.

"We'll do this another time." His lips moved on top of mine. "Love you, gorgeous."

With him gone, I sat on the couch, unable to sleep, my mind—and heart—full of Jem and contradictory feelings I didn't want to have, but were there nevertheless. Why couldn't he have just stayed in Europe? Why couldn't I move on? Why was life so complicated?

Chapter Four

Old Wounds and Magic

"This is insane."

The word hardly described the madness of what we were doing. In the small copse behind my house, Celia and I stood before a metal trash can lightly packed with photos of Jem and me, and some odd items I had dug up from my memory box. Nothing too valuable, even emotionally; just a few things I picked to appease my crazy sister.

The wind had been whipping everything and everybody for the last few days, and it had not quit yet. I wrapped the flaps of my heavy sweater closely around me in a useless attempt at protecting myself from the punishing wind. "Can we go now? It's cold."

Celia slapped me across the top of my arm. "Of course not. We're not done. We have to set the whole thing on fire." Easier said than done. The lighter had apparently run out of fluid, and after a few failed attempts we gave up. "Shit. What do we do now?"

"We go home, Celia." I couldn't get out of there fast enough, but my sister had other ideas. Digging through her enormous purse, she pulled out a small box with a triumphant grin. Matches. Of course she would have matches in that Mary Poppins purse of hers. "How are you going to light one of those in this wind?"

Celia crouched by the trash can and offered me a wicked smile. "Never doubt Super Celia," she said, bringing back my childhood nickname for her. Bending further, she stuck both her hands inside the can and struck a match. By the sudden flare, I could tell she had been successful. She stood up, wiping imaginary dust from her coat, and we both watched as the small pile of items inside the metal container started to burn. A reeking puff of smoke rose, the acrid scent of burning plastic stinging my nostrils. "See? I have my ways."

I weaved my arm through hers and pulled my baby sister closer. She was nuts, but I loved her. "You're a regular witch." The flames quickly consumed the sparse contents of the can.

"And don't you ever forget that, my sweet Muggle sister." The fire died as quickly as it started and, letting go of Celia, I poured the small container of water I had brought with me over the ashes. "Ever the cautious one, Emily."

I smiled. She was the impulsive one, while I was the think-many-times-before-acting one. Sometimes I wondered if one of us had been switched at birth.

Trash can and ashes carefully disposed of, we left the house and headed to our favorite caffeine spot in town. While I ordered my usual flat white, Celia went for the gigantic latte smothered in whipped cream and chocolate sprinkles. How she kept so thin was an honest-to-God mystery. Celia used to get along famously with Jem because of their common love for everything fattening. We sat down in our usual booth in the Old Bookstore, coffees in hand and a plate of mini pastries in front of us. Through the window we could see people rushing back and forth, trying to get out of the nasty wind and fighting to keep their clothes from flying over their heads. Inside the coffee shop it was warm, and the heat of the mugs in our hands melted the remaining chill away. The comforting smell of the coffee caressed our noses and smoothed out our nerves. It suddenly felt very cozy.

"Are you wearing the potion Marcy gave you?" Celia asked, a big fat white mustache on her upper lip. "I don't smell it."

"That's because I'm not wearing it." I was still seriously suspicious of that greenish goo the witch had given me. After last night's dinner, I had been tempted to wear it but had decided against it. "It'll probably kill me, or at least give me a rash."

The look of disapproval Celia gave me was enough to melt metal. "She may look a little quirky, but she's a very powerful witch." I almost choked on my coffee. "You don't believe me, then? Let's make a bet. You wear the potion and if Jem doesn't leave you alone I will… do your laundry and grocery shopping for a month." That sounded heavenly. There were very few things I hated more than washing clothes and going grocery shopping. "If I win, you have to come with me to an event of my choice." God! That was a tough one. Celia was involved in so many things, there was a very strong possibility I would end up bungee jumping.

After a moment of hesitation, I gave in. "All right, you got your bet. I'll wear the stupid stuff, but if someone dies because of it, it's on your head." She laughed, her shoulders pumping up and down in that funny way of hers. My eyes strayed toward the door, and all the blood suddenly drained from my face. Walking in our direction was Jem.

Everything I had ever felt for him came flooding back in a tidal wave. Totally unaware of the turmoil he was causing in my heart, he sped up, a bewitching smile on his face.

"Emily Rose. Oh my God! Is that you, Super Celia?" He opened his arms welcoming my traitor sister, who in a swift move ran to hug him. "Celia, you look great. So grown-up."

Celia didn't even blink when she met my poisonous glare. "Come and join us, Jem. It's been so long." What the hell was she doing? Inviting him to sit with us as if we were still the best of friends. "Emily and I were just chatting."

In his defense, Jem did throw me a questioning look, as if asking me for permission. I must suck at body language because he sat down with us anyway. "I hope I'm not intruding." *Of course you are, idiot.* "I was going to grab a coffee and go, but now...." The blue of his eyes blinded me for a second, and I found myself nodding my approval.

Not one to be coy, Celia slapped him across the forearm. "What the hell were you thinking, leaving us like that and not a word for years?"

Jem chuckled, his face opening up like a book, a gateway to his soul. "I can't tell you how much I regret my decision back then. If I could turn back time I wouldn't even hesitate. I missed you guys so much."

"Yes, it must have been hell living in Paris," Celia teased with a sly side-glance at me.

"I wasn't in Paris, at least not all the time." Jem twisted his hands on the table. "I was based in Provence the first couple years. Then moved a bit closer to Paris. Got to visit quite a bit, but never actually lived there."

My lips were glued together. I was afraid of opening my mouth, not knowing what may come out of it. Celia had no such qualms. "You lucky bastard. Living the life while we were stuck here in good old USA."

"It wasn't that fantastic," Jem replied, the smile dying away. "It was lonely at best. A volunteer prison of sorts. I really couldn't do much without exposing Tina to danger. She was too scared to go to the authorities, and it still isn't resolved."

"But she let you go?" Celia was once again wearing a thick white mustache and blissfully unaware of it.

"Tina agreed to move elsewhere. I think she was bored, as well. So that gave me a way out even though Tina—to quote her—strongly discouraged me from doing so." Jem was still torturing his hands.

I couldn't hold it in any longer. "Why? Why did she discourage you from leaving?" My eyes stabbed his with what I hoped was fury.

He looked up at me with a mixture of surprise and sadness. "She thinks I may be in some kind of danger by association."

My heart flipped. "Are you?"

His hesitation spoke volumes. "No, I don't think so." His expression said otherwise. "I know nothing about the case. Tina never confided in me."

"Were you offered any kind of protection?" Celia asked, her hand going instinctively to his arm.

"No, Tina never went to the authorities with the case, so we were on our own." Jem covered Celia's hand with his own. "But I don't need it. I'm perfectly safe."

"Really? There's no danger?" Celia asked, her face contorting in genuine concern. She had always liked Jem better than any of my other friends.

Jem laughed and waved his hand dismissively. "No, of course not. She was worried about being left on her own, that's all."

At that moment, I scanned through every memory I had of criminal shows on TV and every episode that focused on witnesses of major crimes. I shivered a bit remembering that it never ended well for the idiot who decided to come out of hiding. *It's fiction, woman, only fiction.*

Was it?

Silence fell for a few moments.

"Your boyfriend looks like a good guy," Jem said suddenly. I choked on my coffee.

"He is," Celia replied for me while I coughed into a napkin. "Dave is the best and loves her to death."

Yes, he wouldn't leave for five years without a word of good-bye.

"I'm glad you have someone, Emily Rose." Why did he look sad, then?

"Am I interrupting something?" Marcy, the witch, was standing by our table looking positively quirky. Her red hair had been teased into an eruption of curls, kept in semicontrol by a wide, red headband. Her glasses, still sliding down her freckled nose, were gigantic polka-dotted frames that made her face look even smaller. "May I join you?"

My deranged sister jumped up and hugged the magical Pippi before directing her into the seat next to mine. "Marcy, this Jem. Jem, this is Marcy." She punctuated her words with a wink.

Marcy had a moment of instant recognition. "Oh, *that* friend! Nice to meet you, Jem, and welcome back to the States." Jem looked lost. Who could blame him? This strange little creature seemed to know a lot about him when he knew nothing about her. "Celia has mentioned you." Jem relaxed a little.

"What are you doing here, Marcy? Didn't take you for a coffee drinker," Celia asked.

"I'm not, but they also have the best oolong in town," she explained, straightening the collar of her polka-dot sweater. She waved at one of the waiters, who seemed to recognize her and waved back. "I come here a lot."

A moment later, she pulled on my sleeve and leaned in. "You must not be wearing it or he wouldn't be sitting here with you," she whispered.

I realized she was talking about her silly potion. "I forgot." A little white lie would prevent her feelings from getting hurt, and save me from embarrassment. "I will wear it next time." If I didn't specify when next time was, was it really a lie?

"Mind you, I don't understand why you want him to stay away," the little witch continued in her hushed voice. "It's obvious you still have feelings for him." I almost jumped off my seat. Thankfully, Celia had engaged Jem in an animated conversation about the pros and cons of being a fugitive from the law—not quite sure why—and Marcy's words reached my ears only.

"I do not!" My emphatic tone made the witch blink and grimace. Was that amusement in her face? "I have never had 'feelings' for him. We were just friends."

"Right. And I'm the Pope's wife." I wanted to throttle her. Good thing I actually liked her. "You'd be better off admitting it to yourself and moving on."

As furious as I was at her, I couldn't deny the wisdom of her words. I was in love with Jem. Always had been, and his five-year absence hadn't changed that. The difference was that I now was in a relationship with an amazing man whom I cared about and loathed hurting. "He will hear you," I said, feebly trying to shut her up.

Jem turned his attention to her. "So what do you do, Marcy?"

Celia beamed. "She's a witch."

An eyebrow shooting upward, Jem stared at Celia and then at Marcy. "A witch? Like a Land of Oz witch?"

Marcy laughed. "If you are referring to the Wicked Witch of the West, then no. I'm more the Harry Potter type of witch, minus the flying brooms."

For some reason, he kept staring at me as if expecting me to totally deny this outrageous claim. I couldn't. "She owns a magic store around the corner from here, Polka Dots & Eye of Newt."

There was a moment of silence as Jem apparently digested the information, and then a loud explosion of laughter. "I'll be damned. I thought I'd seen it all. A real witch, eh?"

"Potions made to order," Marcy added, taking a dainty bite of her pastry. "I have one for just about anything that ails you."

"Do you have something that can erase the last five years?" The question floored me. I knew he wanted to be forgiven, but I didn't realize how bad. "Something to turn back time so I can correct my mistakes."

Marcy smiled, her lips stretching from one side of her tiny face to the other. "Sorry, dude, no magic can fix that. You'll have to find another way of dealing with it."

Jem left first, hugging my sister with his long arms and kissing her noisily on the cheeks. He had to content himself with a friendly wave from me though. I was not anywhere near being able to sustain any physical contact. Marcy left next, making sure to remind me of her green potion if I was really serious about keeping Jem away. "Which I seriously doubt," she added with a grin. Annoying little imp.

By the time I got home I was mentally exhausted. There were such contradictory emotions raging through me that my energy was at a record low. I literally crawled into bed, neglecting to change into my pj's, and closed my eyes, wishing I would wake up to find out this had all been a terrible dream. I'm not sure what I hoped was a dream: Jem's return, or his five-year absence.

***

I had been staring at the bottle of Marcy's potion for a while now. Should I put it on? Should I dump it in the toilet? Did I really believe that Pippi had actual magical powers?

Who was I kidding? No, I didn't believe it for a moment, but that annoying weirdo in me could not totally dismiss the idea. *Just in case.* I replaced the unopened bottle on my sink and, with a last glance at the mirror, I left the bathroom. I was meeting with Dave before heading to my yoga class. It had been a long, frustrating day at work, stuck in meetings all day, discussing data instead of teaching the children who had been entrusted to me. Sometimes I wondered why I had to get a degree in education if all I was doing was sitting around a table "analyzing" numbers.

I grabbed my gym bag and my jacket and left. By now, Dave was already at the coffee shop ordering our warm drinks. I was not crazy about drinking before an exercise class, but both our jobs prevented us from seeing each other a lot. We had to take the few moments we had available to us. My brain kept telling me this was yet another reason I should give Dave a key and ask him to move in. I wasn't listening to my brain.

The pungent smell of coffee and cinnamon hit me as soon as I crossed the threshold of the small café. I inhaled deeply, as if I could get energy and strength from the scent alone. Dave was keeping guard over our steaming mugs all the way across the store. He waved, and I waved back, making my way around the obstacle course of tables and chairs. "Hi,

Dave. Sorry I'm late."

Dave stood up, kissed me lightly on the lips, grabbed the jacket from my hands, and pulled out the chair for me. Grateful for the gesture, I brushed my fingers across his cheek before sitting down.

"I was running late myself," he lied. Ever the gentleman, he was only trying to make me feel less guilty about always being late to our dates. "How was school?"

"Don't ask." I really didn't want to talk about it. Bitterness was still very much alive in my stomach, and I didn't want to sour his day by sharing it with him. "Let's talk about your day instead." Dave was a gardener and landscaper. A few years ago, after his last foray to Afghanistan with the U.S. Marine Corps, he had moved into town and opened his own business. What had started as a one-man operation now employed three full-time workers and a legion of part-timers.

"Awesome." When was the last time he had ever complained about a day at work? I couldn't recall a single instance. His work was also his passion, and it seemed that nothing could mar his enthusiasm and positive outlook on life. I was a little envious at times. My job, even though I was passionate about it, offered me ample occasion to be bitter and negative. "We got a new contract for this spring. This lady wants to totally redo her urban yard. She has a huge budget and is open to some really exciting possibilities. It's going to be amazing!"

He had taken hold of my hand across the small table and was caressing it with his thumb. A little shiver of pleasure went up my arm. Why did I have to be so conflicted about my feelings when this extraordinary, sweet man was so into me?

Stupid heart. "I'm glad you had a good day. Do you want to come to yoga with me today?" He sometimes did, especially after a physically demanding day at work.

"Sorry, sweetheart," he said. "I have to meet with the stamped concrete people in about half an hour to go over something. Next time?"

We said our good-byes and headed in opposite directions. The studio was close by and I didn't have to drive, so I left my Mini Cooper parked in the coffee shop parking lot and walked the short distance to the yoga studio.

My instructor was at the front desk, smiling like always. "Good evening, honey. You look stressed."

I chuckled. "Am I ever. You better have an awesome class today because I sorely need it." I shed the jacket and my Crocs by the door, and unrolled my mat.

I liked the spot right under the big ceiling fan because I was not too fond of heat. Later, the fan would be turned on and I wanted to make sure I would be under it. I sat in lotus position on my mat, waiting for the class to start. I closed my eyes and used those few minutes to meditate a little. I could hear the pitter-patter of people's bare feet coming into the space and the swoosh of unrolling mats. The loudspeakers echoed the chiming of temple bells, soothing my soul, and I felt all my tense muscles relax.

"Em," a voice next to me whispered. I opened one eye and glanced at the culprit of such a breach of yoga etiquette. Everybody knew you were not to talk or make any noise during that meditative time. To my utter irritation, my gaze met a very familiar blue one. What in heaven's name was Jem doing here? "I didn't know you came to this studio."

If I'd known he was going to, I would have avoided it altogether today. I felt as if my personal space had been blatantly violated. This was *my* yoga class, and no one I had trouble with was allowed in it. Was I not clear in the telepathic conversations I had with him?

Thankfully my yoga instructor stepped in at that moment and began the session, preventing me or Jem from saying anything else. It was a far from relaxing class. The simple knowledge that he was within arm's reach on the nearest mat was too unnerving. My skin tingled as if he were actually touching me, and my heart refused to slow down. During a particularly challenging move, the so-called wild thing, I chanced a quick glance at him and immediately wished I hadn't. The years had been very kind to him. When he left, he was still a very young man and, even though beautifully built, still had the body of someone with too much energy, but not enough physical activity to develop muscle. The years of boredom—according to him, of course—must have afforded him a lot of time to work out, because taut muscles roped his thin arms and his shoulders. To my total mortification, I was salivating at the sight of his muscles rippling with the effort of supporting himself on one arm. Suddenly I wished the fan were on already, because it had become unbearably hot.

Try as I may, I couldn't stop my eyes from straying to him every time the yoga poses allowed a peek. The *trikonasana* allowed me a full view of his narrow and tight backside. When the yoga instructor told us to turn to the person to our right and support ourselves on each other for dancer's pose, I almost ran out the door. Our palms pressed against each other's and our faces came so close together, I could feel his warm breath. Even though I was proud of my good balance, I felt wobbly and I knew my legs would not hold me for very long. That's when Jem adjusted his posture in order to support me better, and my heart gave in just a little more. *Traitor.*

After our exchange of *namastes* I hoped I could make a quick getaway, but no such luck. Jem immediately came to my side, that goofy smile of his on his lips and his muscled chest way too visible through the large opening of the tank top. "What a great surprise to meet you here," he said. *You can say that again.* "Do you come here regularly?"

My mouth was so dry I couldn't utter a single word, so I nodded enthusiastically. I started rolling my mat, neglecting to clean it. I could do that once I was in the privacy and shelter of my own place. Taking my cue, he started doing the same. "I found out about this studio from Celia." I was going to kill my sister. One moment she was telling me I needed to keep away from Jem, the next she was feeding him dangerous intel about my daily routines. "I told her I wished there were a nearby studio and she told me about this one. But she never mentioned you came here."

That's because she knew I would have her heart for lunch if she did.

"Celia talked to you?" My voice came out low and shaky. "When did you see her?"

"I saw her at the Hangout last night." It figured. My sister and her bad habits. The Hangout was a pseudoclub where local bands nobody had ever heard of came to showcase their music.

That Celia was at the club on a work night wasn't surprising, but still annoyed me. "We shared a gigantic sandwich. Man, I missed having her as my eating partner. Nobody gets my taste for food like she does."

"She should have been at home resting. She worked early today." I hated that I sounded like a teacher. Being a teacher to my students was fine, but to the man I had loved most of my life? It made me feel old and musty.

"She's young." *Thank you, Jem, for making me feel even older now.* "She needs to sow her wild oats before settling. What does she do for a living?"

"She's a nurse at the local hospital." I still found it hard to believe my baby sister had been put in charge of the care of very sick people. Her supervisor was constantly telling me how efficient she was, but my big-sister syndrome never allowed me to fully believe her.

We were now sliding our feet into our shoes and heading toward the front door, rolled mats under our arms, car keys in hand. "Wow, hard to believe." He held the door for me. "I still remember her in pigtails and chasing you around like a duckling."

I smiled. It was a genuine memory. Celia, who was almost six years my junior, used to follow Jem and me around the house, entranced by our teenage, and later young adult, business. She was an adult now, but I still thought of her as a little girl. I probably always would. "She was the most annoying child in the world." I laughed, forgetting to be mad at him for a moment.

"I thought she was cute," he protested, walking beside me

down the sidewalk. "And she always had excellent taste in food."

"Right, as if greasy burgers and fried pickles are the cream of the crop." A snort came out of my mouth. Leave it to him to bring back that part of me. I had stopped snorting a long time ago, once it was pointed out to me that such noises were unseemly in a teacher.

We were almost by the coffee shop, and I really wanted to run away from him. Being this close was confusing and uncomfortable. I felt as if I were betraying Dave just from the waves of heat that invaded my whole body at the sight of Jem's beautiful blue eyes. "I better go," I said.

"Have a cup of coffee with me before you go. Please." He had taken hold of my arm and his hand burned my skin through the thin layer of my jacket.

"I have to get something to eat and go to bed early. I have to work tomorrow." It was only six thirty and I never went to bed before eleven. The wounded puppy look he gave me was all it took for me to give in. "Okay, I'll have a cup. But I can't stay long." I wished I had brought Marcy's horrible potion with me. At this point I would do anything to keep him at bay.

We slid into the usual booth and ordered. It was warm in there, and the comforting smell of coffee helped me relax a little. "What do you want, Jeremy Peter? Why won't you leave me alone?"

He winced at the words. Good. I was glad I wasn't the only one hurting. "I just want us to be friends again, Emily Rose. I know I messed up, but can't you forgive me? I never stopped thinking of you while I was gone, and I told you already that

I regretted my decision as soon as I landed in Paris. Can't you forgive me? I missed you."

How could I explain to him that it was not that simple? That every time we were together my heart went crazy, and my body heat threatened to burn me alive? How could I tell him that I didn't want to betray the wonderful man I was involved with, and that the simple act of looking at him made me have less-than-appropriate thoughts? How could I explain to him that I was still so much in love with him?

"I forgive you, Jem. But I'm not the same. We are not the same." A deep sadness came over me as I uttered those words. It was true. Both of us had changed. It was too late for us. Too much had happened. "We can't go back. We just can't."

Jem lowered his eyes and then raised them to me again. His blue eyes were shiny and intense. "I don't want to go back. I want to move on. I feel I've been stuck in Park for the past few years, and I want to put my life in Drive again." He looked almost desperate and, in spite of myself, I itched to comfort him. "I want you back in my life."

I couldn't stand it anymore. I jumped to my feet, startling him and inadvertently sending my mug tumbling across the table. With a quick move, he stopped it and got up to join me. "I have to go, Jem." It came out like a plea.

Jem held my hands in his and pulled me closer. I could feel the heat of his body against mine, and I shuddered. What were we doing? I had never been too fond of playing with fire. "Let me go, Jem."

After a moment of hesitation, he relaxed his hold on me and set me free. A little bereft now that his hands weren't binding me anymore, I turned my back and hightailed out of the café before I could change my mind. My heart, beating faster than the flutter of hummingbird wings, tried to jump out of my mouth as I ran to my car in the parking lot.

"Don't go." His voice made me stop abruptly as I fumbled with my key fob. Afraid of facing him, I stood as still as a statue, feeling the heat of his body as he came near, wrapped his arms around my waist, and rested his chin in the crook of my neck. In spite of the chill in the air, I was warm all over and my head automatically tilted toward his. "I was a fool, Emily Rose, for not realizing it was you all along."

His breath tingled on my skin and my heart skipped a beat. What was he saying? "Not all those other girls that I fell—or thought I did—head over heels in love with. It was always you. I was too stupid and too blind to see it." Was he really saying what I thought he was saying? The one thing I had always wanted to hear? The last thing I wanted him to say right now? "I love you, Emily Rose. Please tell me it's not too late for us."

With a gulp, I gathered my wits and forcibly pulled away. "It's too late, Jem." I turned around to face him. "I'm in a relationship with an amazing guy. A guy who was there for me when you were not. I forgive you, but I've moved on. You need to do the same."

Shell-shocked and trembling, I opened the car door and hurled myself inside. From the corner of my eye I watched him walk slowly away, shoulders slumped and head tilted forward. Holding on to the steering wheel as if it were a buoy and I was drowning, I allowed the tears I had been holding for years to flow freely down my cheeks. I had done the right thing, sending him away.

Why did it feel so wrong?

Chapter Five

Love and Potions

Five times I had been asked the same question that day. "Ms. Lambert, what's that smell?"

Curious young eyes looked at me from every angle. "What smell? I don't smell anything." *I will go to hell for lying to these young children.* There *was* a smell, and I knew exactly where it was coming from. But damned if I was going to tell my students what it was! "You need to focus more on your work and less on imaginary smells." *I will definitely go to hell.*

Children are funny creatures. They may be unable to focus on work for more than a few seconds at a time, but when they hone in on something they deem weird there is no detracting them from it. "Ms. Lambert, there *is* a weird smell and it's making my eyes water," Johnny said, wrinkling his nose to punctuate the statement. His eyes did look a little red.

Oh boy! As I expected, Marcy's potion did indeed have some unexpected—and unwanted—side effects. It was not a bad smell, per se, but it was pungent and… unusual. After my last encounter with Jem I was desperate to keep him away, so much so I had dabbed the cursed potion behind my ears and on my wrists before going to work. Now I smelled like a funky hippie at a seventies rave and was quickly losing control over my own class. I glanced up at the clock and sighed as I realized I still had a few hours to go before I could hide from my students or take a long, cleansing shower—whichever came first.

The smell seemed to fade a little as the day progressed, but once in a while I would still notice a student or a colleague sniffing the air, looking for the source of the strange odor. It made for a very long day. By the time I was able to leave, I headed straight to Polka Dots & Eye of Newt. That little witch had some explaining to do.

The same overwhelming exotic smell hit me as soon as I crossed the threshold and I had to stop and scratch my nose. Marcy, her red-haired head low over the counter, didn't even twitch as the bells on the door chimed. "Come on in and make yourself at home. Potions to your left, everything else on the right."

I shook my head in disbelief. She didn't even look up to see who had walked into her store. What if I were a masked criminal there to rob her? "It's me, Marcy," I announced, walking straight to her. Her head popped up and a generous smile stretched across her lips. "I hope I'm not disturbing." Disturbing what? The flies? The store was empty, but I needed to say something polite.

With a big wave of her hand, Marcy said, "No one here

but me and the moths. Come on in." She walked around the counter to display her usual eclectic and colorful outfit. Puffy clouds—or were they sheep?—spotted an intensely pink sweaterdress over black leggings and pink booties. "Do you want some tea?"

Tea actually sounded heavenly after the day of sniffing and odor-related comments I had just had. "Would love to."

She waved me to the small seating area, and I sat down on her comfy overstuffed chair. "So what's up?" I could hear the clinking of china around the corner where her kitchen area hid from view.

"I need to talk to you about this potion you gave me." Around me, wind chimes sang their peaceful tune blown by a ghostly breeze.

"I noticed you were wearing it." Who wouldn't? People across the street could probably tell. "Is it working?" She appeared with two cups of steaming tea and sat in front of me.

"If you mean working as in keeping people away, yes. My students and other staff in school didn't want to be around me much today." Afraid I was being too abrasive, I added, "But I haven't seen Jem yet today, so I don't know."

Marcy giggled. "It's a bit… powerful at first, but it does fade the longer you wear it. I should have warned you to wear it around the house for the first couple days." *You think?* Her curls bounced around her face, a giant black bow gracing the top of her head. "But it is very efficient. It will keep Jem away. Of course…." Her voice trailed off and she stared into space as if going into a trance.

A little nervous about her tone, I reached for my teacup,

almost burning my fingers in the process. "Of course what?"

"It only works if that's what you *really* want." What? I didn't see that clause in our unwritten contract. I had to *want* it? Why would I need it if I wanted it? I would just walk away. "Like most things in life, magic needs motivation behind it to work. If deep down inside that's not what you wish, the magic won't work."

Paralyzed for a moment, I blinked a couple times to convince myself I wasn't dreaming. The young witch was studying me with her big, round brown eyes. There was a sharp intelligence beneath all her kookiness. *Maybe she is a real witch.* I sighed. What did I expect from a stinky green potion? Did I really expect it to work?

"You're still in love with him." It wasn't a question. I choked on my tea and was seized by a bout of unstoppable coughing. Marcy stood up and came to gently tap my back. "Why do you fight it? He's obviously in love with you, too."

Once I got my coughing under control, I stared up at my tormentor in disbelief. "Marcy, not that it's any of your business, but I have a boyfriend."

She shrugged. "So what? People break up for all kinds of reasons. Being in love with somebody else seems to me like an excellent reason for a breakup." Her logic set my nerves on edge.

"Jem left me for five years without a word and before that we were only friends. He never felt anything else for me." Why was I explaining all of this to a stranger? Or was I trying to justify it to myself?

"People make mistakes all the time. It's what makes us human. Whatever happened back then, it's in the past." Marcy was running a very real risk of being slapped. I knew all of that, but none of it helped with the current situation. "I would offer you a fall-out-of-love potion, but such a thing does not exist. Once you're hooked, you can fight it like hell, but all you're going to do is tear out your heart and bleed."

My face was burning in rage or shame—not completely sure which. She was right, of course. That didn't mean I was going to do what she was suggesting. Dave was too much of a good guy for me to drop him like a hot potato, and Jem was too much of a loose cannon for me to just jump into a relationship with him. "Thank you, Marcy." *For being totally unhelpful.* I got up and handed her my empty cup. "I have a lot to think about." And a long shower to take.

What was I going to do about this whole mess? Until Jem's call, that day in school, I was so sure I had put him behind me, the Boy Who Left. Like most things I had ever been certain about, this certainty totally collapsed as soon as I heard his voice and locked my eyes with his blue diamonds. Why couldn't he have realized he loved me before he left with that floozy to Paris? Why had he been so clueless back then? Why had I never told him how I felt? Realizing that I was as guilty, even if only by omission, as he was in this catastrophe, I did the only thing a rational, professional twenty-nine-year-old would do: I ducked into the closest ice-cream shop and ordered a triple-scoop butter-pecan bowl buried in a mountain of whipped cream.

I was digging through the ice cream like an eager archaeologist looking for a precious artifact when I felt a hand on my shoulder. I almost fell off my chair, and half of the spoonful heading to my mouth dripped hopelessly onto the tabletop.

"Sorry. Didn't mean to startle you." The deep voice of my boyfriend made me drop the rest of the precious dairy into the bowl, spoon and all.

Hoping I was not wearing the whipped cream anywhere on my face or clothes, I turned around to face him. Dave stood by me in all his never-ending height, a warm smile on his lips and an amused twinkle in his eyes. "Dave, you caught me at a very delicate moment of Operation: Ice Cream. You could have caused a serious spillage incident." He laughed and once again I was reminded of how wonderful he was, how he never seemed to get upset with me no matter how ornery I was. "Sit down. You're giving me vertigo."

Dave sat beside me, eying my ice cream, now slightly diminished in size but still spectacularly yummy-looking. "That looks great. I think I'll get a cone." Before I could say anything, he stood and walked to the front counter to order some ice cream.

I watched him with longing in my heart. Not the sexual longing I often felt when he was around, but a different kind; a yearning for things to be different, to have for him the feelings I had for Jem. Tears danced in my eyes and I quickly wiped them away before he noticed them. Why did love have to be so complicated? He turned around with a huge sugar cone in his hand and I couldn't help it; I jumped off my seat, ran to him, and clumsily hugged him.

He stumbled backward a little. "Whoa... not that I'm complaining, but whoa...." I heard—and felt—him chuckle, my face still glued to his midriff. "Let's sit down before we cause another serious spillage." So we did, and with no disastrous consequences. He got busy with the cone right away as I watched him, my fingers wrapped around the spoon and my heart twisted in a painful mixture of guilt and warmth. Guilt for my lingering feelings for the one who had left me and warmth for the man sitting across from me, oblivious to my inner turmoil.

My unhappy and oversugared stomach growled loudly as we later walked home. Dave's arm over my shoulders, he often had to slow his pace to give my short legs time to catch up. "Am I imagining things, or are you wearing a new perfume?" Oh no, he noticed!

"I bought it from a little witch who obviously has no business in the perfume world." I giggled softly. I was not going to tell him it was supposed to be a magic potion. "Not very nice, is it?"

"God, no. It makes me want to run away and hide." *Huh? He feels like running? Wrong man, wrong man....* "Are you heading home?"

"Yes, Celia is coming over for dinner so I can help her with this knitting project she's working on. Like I can give her a lot of help." I could knit, but my expertise was so basic it could hardly be called that. I guess, compared to my sister, I had mad skills with the needles. "Where are you going?"

"Meeting with a client. The one with the urban yard project." Was I imagining it or was he avoiding my eye? "Challenging but rewarding. When we're done it's going to look amazing." I hardly doubted it. He could perform miracles with a little grass and a few pots. "I'll walk you to your car."

Celia was already waiting for me at home, a giant ball of yarn sitting beside her on the couch and a bewildered look on her face. "What the hell do I do with these?" She was waving two very thick knitting needles above her head. "I suppose I could go back to our Asian roots and do the stereotypical thing." She gestured as if she were about to stick the needles in her hair.

I laughed. "Leave it to you to make something so simple look so hard." I left her struggling with the implements and went into my room to change. "What exactly do you want to knit?" I yelled, sliding into a pair of comfy yoga pants.

"Well, I really want to knit this funky hat I saw in a magazine, but I'll probably stick with a scarf." I joined her on the couch, looking at the ball of yarn. "Do you think that's enough yarn?"

I almost choked. "You have enough to knit an elephant's blanket. Your yarn and the size of your needles will make for a quick and easy knit."

I was not kidding about how my sister made easy things complicated. I watched half-amused as she proceeded to tangle up the yarn and then spend the remainder of the evening working out the knots and tangles. By the time she left not one stitch had been made.

Spending time with my sister was always interesting, even if a little frustrating at times. She had an early shift the next day, so she left me with a little time to kick back and read. Being a teacher, I read a lot, but not for pleasure. I read tons of children's stories on a daily basis and way too many professional books. There was a romantic read I had been dying to dive into. Curled up on the couch, cup of tea in hand, I prepared myself for an evening of swooning romantic literature.

A soft knock stirred me from sleep. Damn! I had fallen asleep shortly after opening the book. My students were like little vampires that sucked up all my energy. Who in heaven's name would be calling this late? I glanced at the clock and realized it was only nine thirty. Shit, I was an old woman in the body of a twenty-nine-year-old.

"Who's there?" I asked, peeking through the peephole on the door. Bright blue eyes met mine. "Jem?" I opened the door and stared, annoyed, at him. "What do you want, Jem? It's late."

"It's only nine thirty, grandma." He stared into my eyes with that boyish manner of his, and my heart fluttered in my chest. "Can I come in?"

I wanted to say no, but then again, a conversation with Jem at the door would attract the curiosity of my neighbors. Ms. Larson, from next door, was a terrible gossip who wrote for the community newspaper. Anything she heard would surely end up either on the pages of the circular or on Facebook. I waved him in.

"What's that smell?" I had never got around to taking a shower. I guessed the offensive smell still lingered.

"Sorry, a bad perfume I bought." I wrapped the cotton sweater around me and headed to the living room.

"Bad? I think it smells wonderful." That was priceless. The man I was trying to push away actually liked the smell.

Good job, Marcy. "You should wear it more often. It smells of the ocean and open skies." What was wrong with his nose? It smelled like old burnt incense, at best.

"You need to stop following me around like this." We sat on the couch, a couple of feet apart. Jem's sunny-sky eyes were glued to mine and I shuffled, uncomfortable under his stare. "You shouldn't be here, Jeremy Peter." The use of his full name no longer seemed to irritate him, for he smiled at me then, a generous, boyish smile that turned my heart to putty. "Stop that!" It came out before I could stop myself.

"Stop what?" He tilted his head like a bird, unaware of his charm. Or was he?

"The smiles, the looks… all of it, Jem. It's not fair to me or to Dave." I sounded so pathetic I think I threw up inside my mouth a little. *Grow a pair, girl.* "You have to stop this little game you're playing, Jem. Please."

To his credit he did look a little remorseful, a shadow crossing his eyes and his sunny smile turning into a frown. "I'm not playing games, Emily Rose. I found out too late that it was you I loved all along. I wasted five years, thanks to my stupidity, and now all I'm doing is trying to regain some control over my life again." He looked down at the floor for a moment. "If you don't feel the same, I'll leave you alone."

"I told you that already." I sure hoped my heart was the liar here. "I'm in a relationship now and there is no room in my life for you anymore."

"That's not the same as saying you don't love me." That simple statement, punctuated with a stab from his piercing eyes, made me wince. He was right, of course. Not that I was ready to admit it to him or myself. "Look me in the eye and tell me you don't love me, and I will leave you alone forever."

Stubbornly, I stared him in the eye, my mouth twitching to say the words my heart wouldn't allow me to utter. For a moment it was as if we had gone back to our childhood when we used to play staring contests. Back then he always won because I never seemed to be able to look into his sweet, handsome face without smiling. I wasn't having any better luck this time. I so wanted to say the words, but the words wouldn't come. Instead, tears climbed up from my heart and danced in my eyes, much to my frustration.

Jem jumped from his perch on the couch and knelt in front of me, covering my hands with his. "Sorry. Didn't mean to hurt you. Forget I said anything. This can't be easy for you." His voice was soft and mellow, like honey to my ears and my heart. In spite of myself, I laced my fingers through his and held on for dear life. "I love you, Emily Rose, and I know I hurt you when I left. I will give you as much time as you need to get over being angry for what I did and be my friend again. I need my best friend. Okay?" I nodded my agreement like the fool I was. "Don't cry. I will leave now. But before I do, Em...." He paused, hesitated for a nanosecond, and planted a soft kiss on my cheek before whispering into my ear, "You should use that perfume more often."

Chapter Six

Phones and Thugs

Dave had been in a hurry to get to his job and left me more than a little annoyed. I wanted to be with him, renew my resolve to stay with him in spite of what my heart was telling me. His delicious kisses and warm, protective arms could change the will of my heart, I was sure of it. But lately he was a little distracted by his work, always running off somewhere, forever putting distance between us. *Damn you, Dave*!

I walked aimlessly down the street. I had planned to spend some time in Dave's arms this afternoon, listening to his sweet whisperings as we curled together on my couch. Now that plans had suddenly changed, I was lost. I could go home and read. God knew I hadn't done much of that lately. A yoga class may be therapeutic, but I hadn't brought any gear. Celia was working, and I didn't feel like sitting alone in the coffee shop.

I found myself walking through the now familiar door of Polka Dots & Eye of Newt.

"Well, hello there, stranger," I heard the melodic voice of the little witch say. Where was she? Scanning the store, I finally found her. Correction, I found her disembodied head on one of the shelves. It scared the crap out of me until she moved and I realized she had been standing behind it. I let out a loud sigh of relief. "You look a little spooked."

That was a serious understatement. My heart had jumped to my mouth and back down again, and I tried to regain my regular breathing. "I thought…. Never mind. Are you busy?" The store was empty as usual. I wondered if she ever did any business.

"You came at the right time." When was it *not* the right time? "Tea?"

"No, I'm okay. I just had some coffee with my boyfriend." I sat down on the couch, and Marcy came to sit beside me. "I was in the neighborhood, and I thought I would come and ask you something."

She gave me a huge smile, her eyes twinkling behind the big-framed glasses. "You are always welcome here, sweetie. What can I do for you today?"

"Marcy, what does it mean when someone really likes the smell of the potion you sold me?" Until that moment I hadn't even known I was going to ask. However, if I were honest with myself, that question had been hanging on the tip of my tongue since I last had seen Jem, almost a week ago. True to his word, he hadn't shown up since then.

Her smile widened. "But that's wonderful! Dave liked it, then?" Why was she assuming it was Dave? "I'm glad I was wrong. That means he is the one your heart truly wants."

Shit! No, no, no, this was not good. "Only your heart's true desire will perceive that scent as being something wonderful. Ahh, the power of love is truly amazing." Her eyes had gone all misty. Damned if the red-haired witch was not a hopeless romantic.

"Unfortunately, Marcy, Dave was not the one who thought it was great." Why was I telling her this? "Dave thought it was awful."

Her smile fell and she tilted her head a little. "Then who?" A surprised look of realization crossed her face. "Oh no, it was Jem, wasn't it? So, I was right after all." She took my hand. Her fingers were cold, but her touch was soothing. I was not feeling too happy right now. "I'm so sorry. I know how much you wanted it to be Dave. But our hearts have a mind of their own and we can't pick and choose whom we fall for."

I wanted to cry or smack myself over the head for being so stupid and believing in that superstitious crock, but deep down inside I knew there was truth to it. I had never really fallen out of love with my best friend. I did love Dave very much, just not the way I loved Jem. I hated myself at that moment, and I hated that I felt so miserable. Tears started rolling down my cheeks.

"Well, Marcy, thank you for trying." Holy crap, was I really sobbing?

Marcy enveloped me with her skinny arms, her fuzzy pink sweater tickling my nose. I worried that I would get that soft garment wet and sticky with my crying snot. Nonsensically, that made me cry even more. "You'll be all right. Everything will turn out okay." The witch's sparkly voice had toned down somehow, and I began to relax. "Good girl. Here are some tissues."

My hands packed with soft tissues, I blew my nose hard and loud. "I have to make a choice." I was speaking more to myself than Marcy. "It won't be easy, but I must choose." Her wild red hair bounced back and forth as she nodded. I blew my nose again and stood up. "I will go straight to Jem's house and tell him I never want to see him again."

Marcy blinked. "Are you sure that's what you really want?"

"Absolutely!" I grabbed my purse and headed for the door, my step quick and steady. "I need someone I can trust, who won't leave me. Someone who will be by my side always. Thank you, Marcy. You've been a great help."

From the corner of my eye I saw her pull out her cell phone and dial a number. The future waited, so I didn't stop to think whom she might be calling in such a hurry. I broke through the daylight outside and walked resolutely to my car. I was going to drive to Jem's place and tell him my decision.

I hadn't been in this part of town since I had moved out of my parents' home. As soon as I signed the lease for my first apartment, my mom and dad put the house on the market, sold it incredibly fast, and following the stereotype they so abhorred, moved to Florida. It was strange to be back in the old neighborhood. It hadn't changed much, and the simple knowledge that my best friend was back made it seem like I was taking a drive down history lane. I parked the car out in the street. There was a black car taking most of the driveway. I couldn't imagine Jem driving that old-fashioned Cadillac. And with tinted windows! What was he thinking, buying that kind of car? It didn't go with his personality at all.

It was odd that Jem had moved into his parents' home. His mom and dad had followed my own into the land of the pink flamingo, but had decided not to sell the house. They had rented the place off and on for the few years it had been vacant, but I had lost track of whom—if anybody—was living there. I walked up the concrete path to the front porch and was surprised to see the door was ajar. *Leave it to Jem to fall back into his old ways.* His mom often complained about his carelessness and total disregard for safety. I chuckled under my breath, remembering the tongue lashings he used to get because of that.

Hesitantly, I pushed the door open just enough to peek inside. Should I go in? I took a few hesitant steps in the foyer and called Jem's name softly. No reply. Yeah, Jem was still messy. There was an overturned coat and umbrella stand, and a tote bag had fallen off the wooden bench, its contents scattered on the rug. Men! The distant sound of muffled voices reached my ears and, without thinking, I stepped inside the house, closing the door behind me. Following the voices, I padded across the hallway toward the kitchen, trying to hear what was being said. Jem was not alone. I could hear at least two male voices furiously talking in hushed tones, but I couldn't tell whether Jem's was one of them.

By the time I was facing the closed kitchen door, I realized that the two voices I heard were not his. *He must be entertaining friends*—and by the looks of the car parked outside, wealthy ones to boot. I almost turned around and left, but if I didn't talk to him now I would likely get cold feet later and never do it.

Coming to a decision, I wrapped my hand around the handle and pushed the door open. "Jem, I need to talk…." My voice died at the sight of Jem, gagged and trussed up like a turkey, sitting on a kitchen stool. The two men flanking him looked up at me in surprise, and I froze. Stupid move, as it turned out, for the two *Men in Black* lookalikes bolted in my direction and, before I could turn around and run, they had me by the arms.

"What the hell are you doing? Jem, what's this?" Again, stupid of me; my ex-friend stared at me with wild eyes, thrashing on the stool, trying to free himself from the ropes that tied him.

Next thing I knew, a sweaty hand covered my mouth and nose and pulled me against one of the men. It smelled of onions and something sour. The girl I thought I had left in the past suddenly surfaced, and I did what I had done at the age of ten when someone tried to take my puppy away from me; I buried my vampire-sharp teeth into the gag-inducing flesh of the man's hand. He wailed, his voice as eardrum piercing as a siren, and he let me go. I bolted for the door, but his partner in crime grabbed one of my arms and held me in place with a viselike hold. The wooden handle of a broom caught my eye. I thrust my free arm out and, tightening my hand around it, I swung it wildly, hitting the two men square in the chest. *Damn, I was aiming at the head. Why am I so short?*

"Ouch, son of a bitch! This one is a wild one." The broom was yanked from my hand, and soon I was just as tied and gagged as Jem was. I was so mad and frustrated that I forgot to be scared. That would come later, once the adrenaline wore off. "Now we have to take this one, too. Damn!"

The two hulks threw both of us over their shoulders like sacks of potatoes and carried us outside where they unceremoniously stuffed us into the trunk of the car. *Is no one watching this?* There we were being carried away like turkeys for the Thanksgiving table, and no one in the neighborhood saw it. *Unbelievable.*

More adrenaline pumped into my veins as I lay in a fetal position, Jem's shoes on my face. I jerked a little and, by the sound of the muffled groans, I must have hit Jem's face with my shoes. We were like two sardines in a very tiny and very hot can.

The car started and, for what felt like an eternity, it jolted and thrust both of us against each other. I was going to be all black and blue. That was, if we were going to see another day. The adrenaline seemed to be waning and fear was creeping in, a trickle at a time. When the car finally came to a stop, so did my heart, it seemed. What was going to happen now? And for that matter, why had those men kidnapped us?

The sunshine blinded me when the trunk popped open, and hands roughly pulled us out of the car and carried us into a building nearby. I took a good look around. I watched a lot of mysteries on TV and I knew it was important to have a good idea of our surroundings if we were to run for it. I had no idea where we were. The area was devoid of any special markers other than the red building in front of us—a small barn, maybe. Everything else was covered in tall beige grasses that waved in the breeze like boneless ghosts, punctuated here and there by a solitary tree.

The building turned out to be storage of some sort. They carried us through a short corridor into a large room, empty besides some old furniture and a few boxes. We were dropped like trash bags on a bed and our gags painfully removed. I would never look at waxing the same way again. I looked at Jem, who seemed as stunned as I felt.

"No point in yelling for help," one of the hulking men said, the gun in his hand pointed at us. "We're in the middle of nowhere, and the walls of this building are insulated and thicker than the Pentagon's. So if you really want to scream, knock yourselves out, but if I were you I'd save it." Without any further explanation, he cut the ties off our wrists, turned around, and left with his partner, closing the heavy door behind them.

The light coming from the dirty skylight inundated the room with a sickly hue that offered very little comfort. I felt spent.

"Let me untie the ropes from your ankles." I figured that doing something—anything—was better than sitting there wondering what exactly had just happened. I rolled off the bed and fell onto my knees to fight with the tight knots around Jem's ankles. He was very quiet. "Aren't you going to say anything?"

Ankles freed from their ties, Jem got on his knees and proceeded to untie mine. "What were you doing in my house, Em?"

I bristled. "So it's my fault that this happened, is it?"

Jem waved his hand. "No, of course not. I only wish you

hadn't shown up when you did. Now I've dragged you along into this mess."

I rubbed my achy ankles and stared at him. "What *is* this mess exactly? What the hell happened?"

Jem leaned back on the bed, legs stretched in front of him, and brushed his unruly curls away from his forehead. "They think I know where Tina is and they want to make sure I tell them." My heart skipped a beat. "We're in big trouble, Emily Rose. Huge."

Like an idiot, I just stared. Words were stuck in my throat and refused to come out. What the hell had I got myself into? And all because of this birdbrained crush I had on my best friend. I sputtered a little and then gave up on saying anything, choosing instead to swat Jem.

He recoiled and raised his arms to protect himself from the surprise attack. "Stop, Em! What the hell are you doing?"

"I hate you, Jeremy Peter," I yelled while whacking him across the chest and shoulders and hating myself for having such a weak punch. "You brought me into this mess. I was fine before you came back."

Jem managed to grab my hands and stop me from hitting him again. I struggled against his hold, but he was stronger. Soon, he had pulled me against his chest and wrapped his arms around me. "Stop, Em. I'm sorry. I really am. I never thought this would happen or I would have never come back here."

My voice, muffled by his soft cotton T-shirt, felt like it was coming from someone else. "I was happy, Jem. I have a great boyfriend, an awesome job…. I had everything under control, and then you show up and totally mess things up for me. Why did you do it? Why?" Tears burned in my eyes, and I rubbed my face on his shirt in a futile attempt to hold them at bay.

I felt Jem's hand brush over my head in a comforting caress, and my traitorous heart quivered a little. "Because...." His voice was soft and barely audible, his breath blowing a few strands of hair into the side of my face. "Because I realized I love you. I've always loved you. I just didn't know. I was too young and stupid to understand how I really felt about you, always chasing the excitement of new faces, new girls. I'm sorry, Emily Rose. The last thing I want to do is put you in any kind of danger."

I sniffed, getting a sick satisfaction in messing up his T-shirt with my mascara. "Well, you did a very poor job at that." An unexpected chuckle rose to my mouth and came out before I could stop it. "A really *bad* job."

A rumble started under my ear, and I pulled away enough to see him laughing, his head thrown back in amusement. "God, I missed your sense of humor." Still holding me close, Jem deposited a kiss on the top of my head and let me go. "I'm really sorry. When Tina told me this was a real risk, I thought she was trying to scare me into staying in France. It looks like she wasn't kidding after all."

I wiped the smudged mascara off my face with the back of my hand. "I must be a vision right now." I giggled a little, inordinately glad I had found a tissue wadded up in my pocket.

"You always look beautiful to me." Argh, why did he insist on being sweet when I wanted to hate him so badly? I wiped my eyes and my face, finishing it all off with a loud blow of the nose. Maybe if I looked a little disgusting he would change his mind. "What are we going to do?"

A quick look around told me what I already knew: it didn't look like there was any way out of this place. I was not one to give up though. I jumped to my feet, trying out my half-numb legs, and walked around. "Come on, let's explore. I'm sure there's something we can do."

Jem laughed again but didn't get up. "I love your optimism, but those guys aren't fooling around. They wouldn't leave us here with our hands untied if they weren't sure that we're stuck."

"Really? You're just going to sit there and do nothing?" I gave him the look I often threw at my sister when she came up with some of her insane ideas. "What a wimp!"

That got him. Standing up quickly, he walked toward me. "You really think we can get out of this mess?"

I turned around to face him again. "What exactly did they say at the house before I got there?"

"They said they knew I was in with Tina and that they couldn't afford to have a loose cannon on their hands." Jem knitted his eyebrows and licked his oh-so-luscious lips. *What is wrong with me?* "One of them said they were going to 'sit on this one' until they figured out what best to do. Did you see their size? They could snap us in half if they decided to."

Jem had some muscles on him and he could probably take one of them, but two? Doubtful, I had to admit. "At least we know they aren't ready to do whatever it is they end up doing to us." Miss Optimistic, my sister always called me. "Do you know anything?" I eyed him, an eyebrow raised.

"No, I know nothing at all." He sighed. "I made sure Tina

never confided in me. Not that she would anyway," he added under his breath. "Hell, what a freaking mess!"

My bra vibrated, making me jump in surprise. Turning my back on Jem, I slid my hand inside my shirt and removed my cell phone. "It's my sister."

Jem's eyes opened wide, and his mouth fell open in a comical way. "Where the hell did that phone come from?"

I pointed at myself while answering the call. "Celia? So glad you called—" Jem crossed the space between us in a long stride and snatched the phone from my hands. "Hey, I was talking to my sis."

"Are you insane? Why didn't you tell me you had a phone on you? How come those guys didn't find it?" Too many questions, too fast. He waved the phone over his head like a lunatic, and I stretched my hand out to him with a not-so-happy look. "Where did you have the damned phone?"

I could hear the voice of my sister from a distance. "I forgot I had it. I always keep it tucked in my bra so I don't have to carry it." I stretched my hand out again. "Can I please have the phone back?"

Reluctantly, he gave it to me. "Un-freaking-believable! You are totally nuts." He used to be much nicer before his French adventure. He walked to the bed, sat down, and dropped his chin to his chest, shaking his head.

"Celia, are you still there?" My sister sounded frantic on the other end of the line. "Listen, something happened…." I gave her a brief report on what had transpired since I left Marcy's store that afternoon. "We're somewhere in the middle of nowhere and those guys are coming back anytime to *deal* with us. We need help."

"What is Jem doing? Is he okay?" my sister asked.

I threw a quick glance at my ex-best friend, still sitting on the bed, mumbling to himself. "I think he may have lost his marbles."

"I did not lose my marbles!" Jem stood up and strode to my side, yelling at the phone. "Your sister has gone mad, Celia. Kookier than the Mad Hatter."

"I can tell you guys are getting along famously." Leave it to Celia to focus on the wrong thing. "So, should I call the police?"

I bit my tongue. Really? Did she even have to ask? "Of course, Celia. I'll leave the phone on so they can track it." Then, as a thought occurred to me, I added, "And let Dave know, please."

Two very blue orbs were fixed on me when I stuffed the cell phone back into its hiding place. "You've always been weird, beautiful." Now what did that mean?

In spite of myself, I felt my legs go a little wobbly underneath me and I took a seat next to him on the bed. The *only* bed in the place. Hell, no. I was not going to share that bed with Jem. No way. I squeezed my eyes shut and conjured my child self in a litany of prayers. *God, please make the police get here before we have to sleep. Or knock me out completely.* I could feel my resolve to tell Jem I didn't want him in my life dissipate quickly. I needed to get out of there.

***

The police didn't come to rescue me from the cruel fate of having to share a bed with Jem. I would have to have a little chat with the Chief of Police about this lack of immediate action. The possibility of death was a very real threat hanging over our heads. The possibility of me losing control and giving in to my lustful instincts even more real and threatening. *Damn you, cops, and your slow GPS trackers!* It happened so fast on TV. Why couldn't it be that quick in real life?

The night had fallen so suddenly it felt as if someone had switched off the lights. The building was suddenly immersed in dusky light from the full moon outside. We had found a small lamp behind a box and could at least see each other and our immediate surroundings. Further exploration had uncovered a small half bathroom with running water, a box of water bottles and granola bars, and boxes full of junk that neither belonged or would be in any way useful to us. We had exhausted all possible distractions from the fact that there were two of us and only one very small bed.

At first we sat gingerly side by side, munching on the stale granola bars and sipping water from the bottles. Talk was scarce and awkward. We seemed to have reverted to being young teenagers on a first date. I looked up and saw the full moon peeking down on us, as if mocking our discomfort. "All we need now are some werewolves to come and scratch on the door."

Jem looked at me as if I had gone crazy—which I probably had. "Werewolves?" I pointed at the round cheesy face of our moon, and he chuckled. "I see. I think we're safe from them inside here."

But was I safe from him? Or at least from this overwhelming pull he had on me? I didn't trust myself. *Think of Dave, think of Dave, you foolish girl.*

A glance at my watch told me it was nearly eleven o'clock. My eyes were starting to droop, but I didn't want to be the first one to give in. "Are you tired?" I asked him with a sideways look. As if on cue, he yawned. "I guess you are."

"I'm going to shut my eyes for a while." He crawled on top of the bed and made room for me beside him. "Come on, you need to rest." *Oh my God, this is it!* The moment I was dreading. On one hand, I cringed at the idea of lying there, Jem spooning me as if we were lovers. On the other, I was looking forward to it a little too much. Hesitantly, I swung my legs up on the bed and allowed my back to align with Jem's long body. The small cot wouldn't allow any decent space between us.

Jem draped his arm over me after pulling the threadbare throw to cover us. I lay stiffly, practicing my shallowest breathing so my body didn't move at all. I could hear and feel Jem's slow breathing on the back of my head. He had fallen asleep. When the cell phone vibrated in my bra, I almost jumped out of my skin. "Celia?"

"Yes, it's me. Are you okay?" My sister's voice was a balm to my soul. Until that moment I hadn't realized how scared I really was, distracted by the whole Jem factor. "The police want to talk to you."

I was whispering, hoping not to wake Jem up. A sleeping Jem was so much easier to resist. "I'm okay. How come the police haven't located us yet? It's been hours."

The voice from the other end was not my sister's anymore. "Miss Lambert, we are having trouble with the GPS signal."

"What do you mean? Did you try to… triangulate the signal or whatever it is you do? I have a perfect phone signal." I realized I sounded slightly desperate. I must have drained the last of the adrenaline the last time I had used the bathroom.

"Something is jamming the GPS signals." I whimpered. "Don't worry. All this means is that it will take a little longer to locate you guys. We're thinking you must be close to a military facility of some kind. Just like we can track GPS signals, we can as easily track a jammer. Hold on tight for a little longer."

My voice shook and so did my arms. "What if *they* come back before then?" I didn't really want to hear the answer, but I had to ask. Reality was now beginning to sink in. "They'll kill us."

"Did they leave you any food?" Nice of the officer to be concerned about our nutritional health, but weird time to ask that question. "If they left you food it means they expect not to come back for a while."

"They left a box of granola bars and water bottles. Not exactly a gourmet meal." I laughed nervously, trying to make myself feel better.

"We will get you out of there before they come back." I liked that he seemed so sure of himself. "You and your boyfriend relax and we will be there before you know it."

"My boyfriend? Jem's not my boyfriend." Had they even contacted Dave? I heard Celia on the other end again. "What did you tell the cops about Jem and me?"

"Nothing," she said defensively. "He just assumed. How are you guys doing, anyway?"

"Don't change the subject. Where's Dave?"

"I tried to call him, but he never answered his phone." Had she really tried? "I'll try again after I get off here. Em…?" What now? That tone always promised trouble. "Marcy told me about Jem's reaction to the potion. Why do you fight it if he's the one you really love?"

So that's who Marcy was calling when I left the store. "I don't want to talk about it. Find Dave and tell him what's going on. I'm getting off now." I hung up, furious at Celia and Marcy. And where in heaven's name was Dave? Why wasn't he answering his phone? And why were my legs and arms shaking so hard?

"Are you okay?" Jem's groggy voice reached my ears with the silkiness of a caress. His arm tight around me, he pulled me closer to him. "You're trembling. Are you cold?" I had been running on adrenaline since I had first set eyes on the two thugs who kidnapped us. Not anymore. My whole body convulsed and ached. I was suddenly terrified. "Sweetie, we're going to be okay."

Before I could do anything about it, Jem had turned me around to face him. We were so close I could feel the warmth of his breath on my face. Supporting his weight on one arm, Jem hovered over me, and the air became thick and hard to inhale. It was dark, but I could clearly see his amazing eyes glisten, as if they had a light of their own. Or maybe it was just my hyperactive imagination fueled by the yearning growing alarmingly fast within me. If he was going to say something, he thought better of it and silently drank me in. I must have done the same, for I was positively starting to feel the alcohol-like effects of his eyes on mine, his hand on my cheek, his thumb distractedly rubbing against the corner of my lips. Reality was losing definition as I dove deeper and deeper into Jem's brilliant eyes.

The phone vibrated against my breast once again, and I realized our faces had been moving toward each other like magnets. A moan of disappointment echoed through the dark room, and I wasn't sure whether it had come from me or him. The phone now between the two of us, I made myself look away from his handsome face. "Hello," I said after clearing my throat of the huge lump that had developed there. "Who's this?" Jem hadn't moved an inch.

"It's the police, Ms. Lambert." Score for the cops! They may not be there rescuing us, but the phone call had almost certainly stopped something I would have regretted later. "I'm afraid we are having a lot of trouble locating you and your friend. I wanted to let you know you should prepare yourself for the possibility we may not get to you before the kidnappers return."

I sat up so quickly I bumped my head against Jem's lip. He jumped out of the bed, covering his mouth and cursing.

"Ouch!" I rubbed my forehead furiously. That was going to leave a mark. "What do you mean, prepare ourselves?"

"Look around you. Find something heavy or sharp that you can use as a weapon. Just in case." Who was he kidding? If the thugs had even suspected there was something in there we could use against them, they would have never untied us.

"Something… creative, maybe." Did he want us to paint something or carve a weapon out of the bed? *Wait! The bed has decorative metal rods. If I can unscrew the headboard and remove the rods, we may just have an improvised weapon.* "Do you see anything you could use?"

"Yes, maybe. Thank you." With the promise of another call as soon as he had any news, the police officer hung up. A little beeping sound came from my phone.

"What's that?" Jem asked, walking around to my side of the bed. He looked so sexy as he touched his lip with his fingers. Another inappropriate thought invaded my brain. I shook it off.

"The battery is dying." His eyes widened and I noticed his lip was a little swollen. "Crap, sorry. Does it hurt?" I stood and crossed the space between us to examine his lip. I had to stand on my tiptoes, but I was able to confirm I had busted his lip. A trickle of blood rolled slowly down toward his chin. Using my finger I wiped it away.

I shouldn't have done that.

The heat was back in force, and I was pretty sure I wasn't the only one feeling it. Jem had taken a step closer to me and my hands were caught between us, lying flat on his hard chest. "What are you doing?" Deep ocean eyes drowned me, and the panic I always felt around him dissipated as if by magic. All I could think of was his eyes, and all I could feel was the growing warmth enveloping me whole.

"God, I missed you." His voice, low and hoarse, caressed my ears. My legs buckled, and I held on to him as if my life depended on it.

His swoonworthy lips descended on mine, and I got lost in the taste and scent of him. It had been a lifetime since our mouths had explored each other like that. Even then, I was the only one who had been fully conscious—considering he had been sleeping at the time. It was exactly like I remembered it. Better even, now that I knew Jem to be as into me as I was him. Shamelessly, I pulled him even closer, wrapping my arms around his waist and deepening the kiss. I couldn't— wouldn't—have any space between us. I had waited too long for this moment, and all that pent-up desire had suddenly exploded out of the deepest corners of my body and soul.

With a stumble, Jem pushed me onto the bed. We fell on it with a big screeching of old wood against metal, me on top of him. "I think we may have broken the bed," he whispered against my lips.

Busy trying to pull his T-shirt over his head, I giggled absently. His glorious chest was now bare, and I felt my whole body turn to hot, thick liquid. I flattened my hands across the muscles of his torso and stopped for a moment, frozen by the overwhelming feelings taking control of me. His mumble reminded me that the T-shirt was still around his neck, covering his face, and I reached out to remove it completely. His beautiful, genuine smile hit me harder than if he had slapped me. What was I doing? I had a boyfriend. Whom I loved. Dearly.

"You okay?" Jem asked, worry clouding his eyes.

I jumped off him and walked a few steps away from the bed. "Hell no! I can't do this." I wasn't sure whether I was speaking to Jem or myself.

Bare-chested and obviously confused, Jem rose to a sitting position and threw me an inquiring glance. "What can't you do?" Oh God. He was so gorgeous, and my mind went back to his lips and how they had tasted like ambrosia. I took two more steps away from him.

"Put the shirt on, Jem." Try as I may, I couldn't take my eyes off him, a mess of blond curls and swollen lips. "I'm in a relationship. I must be mad. We must be mad."

He looked so forlorn I felt I needed to give him a hug. Instead, I turned my back on him and pulled out my phone. "But, Em—"

"Jeremy Peter, here we are being held captive by God-knows-who—someone who will probably have us killed soon—and we're all over each other like crazed rabbits." The image of mating rabbits made me cringe, right as my phone beeped again in my hands. "Great! And now the battery is pretty much dead."

I half turned just in time to see Jem throwing himself back onto the bed and groaning. I stared at my phone, and then I remembered the new wireless charger Dave had given me for my birthday. It was a flat contraption about the size of a cigarette pack that I could stuff pretty much anywhere and required only a tiny wire.

"What are you doing?" Jem had retrieved his T-shirt and was now sitting on the edge of the bed, sliding it over his head. He watched me curiously as I raised my shirt and pulled out something from under the waist of my jeans. "What's that?"

"A charger." No need for further explanation. I looked around for a flat surface to lay it down on, but finding none, I set it up on the floor with my phone on top.

"You had a charger on you?" Jem sounded almost irritated, as if being prepared was a bad thing. "Is there anything else you have on you? Like maybe a key out of this damned place?"

I actually stuck my tongue out at him, like I used to do when we were little and he pissed me off. God! How immature of me. This man could make me do things and behave in ways I wouldn't dream of with anyone else. To his credit, I was so distracted by his presence I hadn't had much time to think about our less-than-desirable situation.

Not wanting to sit next to him, I ended up sitting cross-legged on the floor. The concrete was uncomfortable and cold, but it beat the awkwardness of feeling Jem's body next to me. It was very late and I was sleepy, but going back to that bed was not an option. Not while my ex-best friend was in it.

Jem had lain back down, his arms crossed behind his head and his legs crossed at the ankles. "Are you going to tell me why? The real reason why you're fighting this—fighting us?"

I snapped my head up and gave him another look of death. "I told you why. I have a great boyfriend whom I very much would like to keep. You, on the other hand, have not been part of my life for a very long time." Ouch! I'm sure that stung a bit, but so be it. He didn't seem to be getting the idea at all.

With a flinch, Jem shook his head. "But you don't love him."

What? Where did he get that idea? Well, we had just almost.... Still. It had been a moment of weakness during a trying time for both of us. It did not mean anything. "I do love Dave." I was outraged by his assumption. "He is a wonderful man and we have been dating now for almost two years."

"If you've been dating that long and you love him so much, why haven't you given him a key to your place yet?" Bang! Right in the kisser.

"It… just never… seem—it never seemed to be the right time. Not because I don't love him." I was whining, and that was so unlike me. *I hate you, Jem.* Only, of course, I didn't.

Jem was silent for a few moments, studying me. "Okay, maybe you love him a little," he finally said, turning on his side and supporting his head on his bent arm. "But I know you have loved me for a long time, Emily Rose. You loved me since we were in college. I know you have."

How did he know? "You are so full of shit, Jeremy Peter. You are pulling at straws, and you know it." I hoped my face didn't betray me, for my heart had started racing again, and my cheeks felt hotter than hot.

His eyes softened. "That day in your room when you thought I had fallen asleep…." My heart thumped like an angry bunny's. "I had fallen asleep for a little while, but I woke up to find you kissing me. Remember that?"

How could I forget my one moment of true insanity? "You were awake?" My feeble response came out so quietly I couldn't be sure he had heard it.

He nodded. "I was so surprised by it I decided to see where it would go. You had never shown any indication you felt like that." His eyes were burning holes into my soul. "And you know what? I found out I liked the feeling of your lips on mine. I found out that I wanted so much more…."

I swallowed bile. Torn between being embarrassed and

being annoyed, I couldn't find the words to express any of my feelings. I sat on the cold floor, staring at the shadowy figure of my ex-best friend, and wishing things were so very different.

"Then it hit me. What if things didn't go well between us? After all, I didn't exactly have a good record when it came to relationships. What if I messed up things with you, as well? I would've lost my best friend. I didn't think I could handle that." He sighed, sat up, and slid his long legs out of the bed. Even in the semidarkness of the room I could see the glint of his perfect sapphire eyes. "I couldn't risk losing you. So I pretended I was dreaming about the flavor of the month."

What did I say to that? How should I have responded? I was so confused. So I went on the attack. "So you decided to move to another country and totally cut communications with me? Sorry, but that doesn't sound like the actions of someone who does not want to lose a friend. It sounds like someone who couldn't care less."

Gripping a fistful of his T-shirt over his heart, Jem bit down on his lower lip. "Don't you get it, Em?" His voice came out tainted by pain, and I squirmed. "I left because I was in love with you. I couldn't handle being around you and not being able to kiss you. I couldn't sleep at night. My dates lasted but a few hours, and—in spite of what you may think—I did not have a slew of girlfriends waiting for me in my bed." I watched his Adam's apple bob. "Shit, Em. I went away so I could save you and me from heartbreak."

We were silent for a while, both staring into each other's eyes. The air around us seemed to crackle with electricity.

"That was the most stupid thing you could have done. How would that save me from heartbreak? I've been hurting for five long years, Jem. How is that better than us dating and failing?" I realized I had just given out too much information, and I bit my tongue to prevent myself from revealing any more. "How did you ever think moving to Europe and spending the next five years with no communication would help us in any way?" I was livid that he thought I was stupid enough to believe this ridiculous reasoning.

He raked his hair with his hand in a move I knew all too well. "I was a dumb, stupid kid. I thought if I moved away for a few months, whatever feelings we had for each other would sort themselves out, and our friendship would remain intact." His voice trembled a little. "God, Em. We were always together, in each other's houses…. Shit, we even shared a bed sometimes. I thought a little distance would allow us to see clearer, figure things out."

"It was five years, Jem. Five freaking long years." I was yelling.

In a swift move, he jumped from the edge of the bed to come and kneel before me, his hands holding my arms. "Tina told me the whole thing would blow over soon." It sounded like a plea. "She told me the prosecution had other witnesses lined up, all the evidence they needed. As soon as the case was taken to court it would be over, she told me. Then both Tina and I would be free to live our lives again as we pleased. I thought I was going to be away for two, three months tops."

I digested what he'd told me, his hands burning the skin of my arms. His mere proximity made me vibrate with yearning.

"What did you expect, Jem?" I finally said. "Did you think I was going to wait for you for years without knowing whether you were alive or dead? I moved on. I had to. I couldn't just sit at home and pine for someone I had no reason to believe cared enough for me."

His hands tightened around my forearms. "Of course I cared," he protested, his eyes seeking mine. "I was your best friend. We had been together since we were kids. How could you doubt I cared?"

Angry, I pulled away from him, freeing myself from his touch. "How could I not? You left me without even saying good-bye. Did I mention the five years of total radio silence? Did you really expect me to wait for you?"

He hung his head, chin and eyes dropped to his chest. "No, I suppose not." Even when I was angry at him, I wanted to hug and comfort him. "I just hoped…."

Making a decision, I stood up, grabbed my phone and charger, and walked toward the bed. "No point in dwelling on this. I love Dave and I am not giving him up because you suddenly materialized in my life again." I made sure to stress the word *love* to see him flinch. I was not disappointed. "There are men who wish us harm and they may come at any time. We should focus on trying to save our skins. Can you help me try to unscrew some of these metal rods from the bed?"

After a moment of hesitation, Jem stood up and joined me by the bed. It was going to be a long night ahead, so we might as well spend it working on a solution for our dire situation. Those rods may very well be our only hope for survival.

***

The phone woke me up. I grabbed it instinctively, still groggy from sleep. "Yes?"

"Are you okay, Em?" The familiar voice of my sister soothed my aching heart.

"So far, we're still alive," I joked, blinking my eyes open. Morning had dawned, and the room was no longer immersed in darkness. I was lying on top of the bed, but where was Jem? I frantically scanned the area and found him stretched out on the cold floor a few feet away from the bed.

"Don't even joke about it." My usually irreverent sister sounded somber and anxious. "The police are still trying to pinpoint your location. With all the technology available nowadays, you would think they'd have found you by now."

"Relax, sis. We're both okay," I assured her, and realized I was assuring myself as well. "They haven't come back yet."

"I talked to Marcy, and she's concocting some spell to help the police find you." Of course, she was. In spite of everything, I smiled. Probably some smelly potion that would drive the detectives up the walls. "She's pretty certain she can do it."

"I probably should get off, Celia." I didn't want to add to her anxiety, and to be honest, knowing the little witch was up to her tricks made me that much more anxious. "In case the cops call."

We said our good-byes, Celia's voice betraying a little sob, and I hung up. I was still lying on top of the bed, turned on my side. Jem still slept, his handsome features twisted into a frown. He was having bad dreams. Was he dreaming about the danger we were in or our personal issues? I knew I should be preparing for the inevitable. Those guys would be coming back at any time, and we should be ready. However, I couldn't move. I didn't want this moment to end. Watching Jem sleep gave me a sense of peace and satisfaction I hadn't felt in a very long while. Weird how I had never felt like that with Dave. In fact, I couldn't remember a single instance when I had watched him sleep. Any time he stayed over, I always went straight to sleep after our lovemaking. In the morning, I was always out of bed and running to get coffee before I even looked at him. Why was that?

Jem stirred from sleep, and his eyes slowly began to open. I sat up before he could see me staring at him like a teenager in love and got busy collecting the two rods we had been able to remove from the headboard. They were heavy and could potentially serve as good weapons. We had come up with a plan, and we agreed that whatever our issues with each other were, they had to wait until we were out of there, safe and sound.

"No coffee?" Jem was sitting now, rubbing his head.

I laughed. "Right. I also made a couple mimosas to go with the quiche in the oven." It was always so easy to kid around with Jem. I missed that more than anything else. Dave was an amazing guy, but his sense of humor sometimes didn't quite match mine, and my silly, sarcastic jokes often fell flat with him.

"The sun is shining. They'll probably come to get us very soon." He voiced my own thoughts. "We should move closer to the door. Not sure how well we'll be able to hear them coming."

We wanted to catch them by surprise. After all, they had guns. We had metal rods. Without the element of surprise on our side, we didn't have a prayer.

We moved to stand by the wall close to the door, each with a rod in hand. My stomach grumbled. I was very hungry.

"Yeah, I hear you," Jem said with a chuckle. "I'm starved myself. You can only eat so many granola bars and handle so much stress before your body starts to rebel."

Didn't I know it. I had spent part of the night locked in the tiny bathroom while my body rid itself of the extra fiber. It had not been my proudest moment. Jem, on the other hand, as used as he was to eating tons of junk food without gaining so much as an ounce, did not seem affected by it at all.

My phone rang again. I quickly answered. It was the detective. "Good news," he said. "We have your location. There are cruisers on the way as we speak. Did you find something to defend yourself with just in case?"

"Yes, we're armed, so to speak." I was too afraid to allow myself to feel relieved yet. "How long do you think until you guys get here?"

Jem raised his eyes to me in a silent question. I nodded.

"Less than forty-five minutes," he replied. "But the bad guys may get there first. So be at the ready." He hung up.

My mouth was dry. I realized I was trembling and Jem, having without doubt noticed it as well, laid a hand on my arm to comfort me. "It will be okay," he whispered. I nodded again.

I'm not sure how long we stood there, not moving much, scared out of our wits. Reality had finally sunk in and my usual proclivity for sarcasm seemed to have vanished. Standing behind me, Jem supported me when my body went boneless and I almost fell backward. His solid, warm chest gave me back some of my strength and, for once, I did not begrudge him the contact.

Both our bodies tensed up as we heard someone turn keys in the lock and open the heavy door. Jem and I had lifted the makeshift weapons above our heads and, as soon as the tall figures of our two kidnappers appeared inside the space, we hit them across the heads as heavily as we could. They both fell to their knees and, with no hesitation, we hit them again. Not waiting to see whether they were conscious or not, Jem grabbed my hand and we took off, running toward their car, parked right outside the door.

"Where are the keys?" I asked, frantic as I realized there were no keys in the ignition.

"It's keyless," Jem said. "We should be close enough to them to…." He pressed the ignition button and sure enough, the engine roared. "Yes! We're in business."

Jem sped out of the open area while I played with the GPS, trying to figure out where we were and where we should go. "Right, turn right," I yelled. "It will take us to the main road."

My phone rang in my bra, and I felt as if someone had electrocuted me. My nerves were on edge. It was the detective again.

"We're out," I told him, my voice a lot louder than it needed to be. "What do we do?"

"Stop at the next gas station and wait for me," he said. "My guys should be coming up soon." Two cruisers with the lights flashing and sirens screaming passed us by on the dirt road just as I hung up. I let out a huge sigh of relief.

Jem stopped at the next gas station, ten minutes up the road, and we decided to stay put. My body was assailed by tremors, and my teeth chattered like castanets. Even though my brain refused to think about what had happened, my body had a different perspective on things. Relief mingled with a tidal wave of all the anxiety I had been holding inside.

"Are you okay?" Jem asked, a worried look on his face. "You're shaking like a leaf." He twisted on his seat to look in the backseat. "No blankets or jackets here. Let's sit in the back."

Without pausing to question his strange request, I opened the door and quickly switched to the backseat, immediately followed by Jem. He scooted closer and wrapped his arms around me. At first, I flinched a little. *What a strange time to get physical.* But then I realized he was only trying to keep me warm, like he used to do on very cold days when we were kids and I had unwisely walked to his house coatless. I relaxed against him and closed my eyes. The warmth of his body soothed my anxieties, and I think I dozed off because the next thing I knew there was a man waving a police badge outside the car.

We stepped outside to meet the detective who had been so diligently working to rescue us. Detective Jarvas introduced himself and shook our hands. Another cop brought us a couple blankets and two cups of steaming hot coffee. Never had gas station coffee tasted that good! With the blankets over our shoulders, we sat on the wooden bench outside the mini-mart and answered every question the good detective asked us. Then he left us to our own devices to go talk to the officers who had just arrived from the place we had escaped from.

"I feel like I'm a character in a mystery novel." Growing up, I used to read a lot of mysteries because my dad was an avid reader of the genre. Being in the middle of one was not nearly as much fun as reading it.

Jem smiled, his blue eyes twinkling like sapphires in the sun. "I half expect Miss Marple to come around the corner."

As if on cue, someone did come around the corner, driving at the speed of light and slamming on the brakes so hard the car weaved to a sudden stop right in front of us. My crazy sister! No one drove quite like her.

"Brace yourself," I told Jem with a little chuckle. "Here comes trouble."

Celia slammed the car door and ran the few feet between the car and us. "Oh my God! Are you guys okay? Did they hurt you? I want to talk to whoever is in charge. I...." The barrage of words kept coming while Jem and I sat quietly, enjoying the sound of a friendly voice and the cold breeze on our faces.

After many hugs and way too many questions, Celia was finally sated. "I'm so happy to see you both, crazy kids," she said as another car, a bright yellow VW Beetle, came to a stop beside her car. "Look, there's Marcy."

What in heaven's name is Marcy doing here?

The little witch stepped out of the car, closed the door,

and walked around to the passenger side, waving at us. She was wearing a short dress in a cartoon print fabric of bright blues and yellows, and bright orange sneakers. Her hair was the usual mess of red curls piled on top of her hair and secured with a huge blue bow.

She approached us with a big paper bag in her hands. "So glad to see you're safe and sound," she said, her glasses hanging on the edge of her tiny nose. "I thought you would be hungry, so I stopped at McDonald's on my way here."

I hated fast food, but that hamburger and fries tasted like nectar from the gods. I hadn't realized how hungry I was until I took my first bite. Jem was in ecstasy. With each bite he took, a groan of pleasure escaped his lips. He sure loved his burgers! I laughed, a great weight finally lifted from my chest, and Jem joined me.

"Thank you, guys." I felt better than I had in a long time, now that I was safe and my stomach was full. Marcy and my sister were still eying Jem and me with some worry, as if they expected us to break down and cry—which I may have done had I not been feeling so happy to be alive. "Where is Dave?" I finally noticed my boyfriend was not part of the welcome committee.

"We couldn't get ahold of him," Celia said with a frown. "I called his work phone. His receptionist told me he was out on a job and to try to call his cell. I called it and no answer. I left several messages, texted him a few times, and nothing. Weird, don't you think?"

It was a bit strange, but he had worked on sites where the phone signal was nonexistent. He would call as soon as he could check his messages, I was sure. "He'll call back as soon as he can."

Jem looked at me with a sideways glance. "So the perfect boyfriend vanishes when he's most needed."

I wanted to slap him, but I had to admit it annoyed me that Dave was absent during such a tough time in my life. "Shut up, Jeremy Peter."

"Well, my young friends." It was the detective again. He had a lit cigarette between his fingers, and a big cloud of smoke followed him. "I've talked to my officers, and we're in a bit of a pickle." He took another drag on the cigarette.

"A pickle? What do you mean?" Jem coughed a little as he inhaled some of the smoke.

"The guys who had you are minions." He frowned as both Jem and I coughed again. He threw the butt on the ground and stepped on it. "Sorry, nasty habit."

Marcy waved her hand in front of her face. "How is that a problem? That those guys were minions?" she asked, pulling out an embroidered handkerchief and covering her nose with it. "You got them, right?"

"Yes, we have them. However, the person who hired them is still on the loose." He stuffed his hands in his pants pockets and rocked on his feet. "The two who kidnapped you are hired muscle. They don't know much and are too scared to tell us who their boss is."

"So what do we do?" Celia asked, munching on some leftover fries.

Detective Jarvas squinted at Jem and me and licked his lips. "It means, young people, that you have to be put into a safe house until we find the culprit."

We both jumped to our feet and exclaimed at the same time. "What? Safe house? What do you mean?"

"Calm down," the detective said. "It won't be that bad. We'll keep you both in a safe house for a few days until we can track down who's behind this."

Speechless, I looked up at Jem, a question in my eyes. He shrugged and looked back at the cop, who had removed a pack of cigarettes from his shirt pocket. "Is that really necessary?" Jem asked.

"Whoever this is, he thinks you guys know where Tina is or that she confided in you, Jeremy." The detective had lit another cigarette and puffed smoke up into the air. "You two are in danger for as long as he's free. So, yes. It is necessary."

I wrapped the blanket tighter around my shoulders. "I'm a teacher. I can't disappear and leave my class by itself."

"We will contact your school and help them arrange for a substitute teacher. A good one, I promise," the police officer said. "It shouldn't be for very long. We have very good leads. I'll leave you to discuss it." He walked away, leaving a trail of smoke behind him.

We sat back on the bench, stealing glances at each other, almost scared to bring it up. "What do we do?" Jem asked finally.

Celia slapped him across the arm. "You go into the safe house, of course," she exclaimed. "What kind of question is that? You guys are in danger."

"Celia, I don't want to be stuck in a strange place again," I protested. "These last few hours were more than enough."

"You won't be a prisoner," my sister added. "And it's for just a few days. You can look at it as a… retreat."

Marcy pushed her glasses up the bridge of her nose. "You're scared of being stuck in a house alone with Jem." *Thank you, Marcy. Helpful as usual.* "Admit it!"

An amused smile appeared on Jem's lips, and I fought the urge to stick my tongue out at him again. "I am not!" I said, a bit too vehemently.

"She's too scared of falling for my charm and wit," Jem said, a silly smile plastered on his face.

"Right! And the Pope is not Catholic." He could still make me feel like a young girl. It wasn't an altogether bad feeling.

The little witch signaled me with a nod. She wanted to talk to me in private. I stood up and followed her a few steps away from the rest. "What is it, Marcy?"

Digging through her gigantic purse, the redhead pulled out a little pink bottle hanging from a chain that she slid into my hands. "Hide it," she said in a whisper. "It's for you, just in case."

I was puzzled. "In case of what?" I asked, looking at the little bottle in my hand. It was a pretty little thing.

"In case you find yourself giving in to Jem's charms," she said, twitching her nose. "You guys obviously have a history."

"Is this another potion?"

"Yes, and a very effective one."

I took a deep breath, gathering the patience to reason with Glinda, the crazy witch. "The other one didn't work at all."

She chuckled. "I beg to differ," she said. "It worked only too well. You weren't honest about your feelings. This one will put him in a daze."

About to argue with her, I stopped. "A daze? How would that be helpful?"

A quick glance at the rest of the group reassured her that it was safe to continue the conversation. "Say you are about to give in to his wiles." *Wiles? Is she for real?* "You have him smell this potion. He will go into a temporary trance, almost as if he were hypnotized. That will give you ample time to remove yourself from the scene."

For once, that actually didn't sound like a bad idea. "Will it hurt him in any way?" I may not want Jem in my life, but I did not want to harm him either.

"No, of course not," she assured me. "It will keep him out of it for five, ten minutes tops. Then it's back to business as usual. Hang it from your neck and keep it with you at all times."

The little red bottle seemed to throb in my hand, but I dismissed that as a figment of my imagination and exhaustion. I slipped the bottle into my pocket. "Thank you, Marcy. Hopefully I won't have to use it."

"If that doesn't work, we can always feed him a red lizard's tooth...."

And just like that, we were back to crazy.

Chapter Seven

Hideouts and Regrets

The safe house turned out to be a small cabin in the woods with a mother-in-law suite—an attachment to the main building where the officers babysitting us would be staying. "That way you still have your privacy, but we can be close enough if needed," Detective Jarvas had explained.

Much to my dismay, there was only one bedroom in the house. "But there are two of us," I protested.

"Your sister told us you guys were a couple," one of the officers said. I was really going to kill my sister. "Anyway, there are two beds. No harm, no foul."

Jem and I were promised burner phones to keep in touch with family, and we were allowed to pack some of our things. Celia had promised to send us a care package soon.

"There will be new books and some junk food in it," she said with a mischievous smile. Then she had lowered her voice and whispered for my ears only, "And maybe a potion or two." Little devil, that's what she was! She was enjoying the fact that I was stuck with the one person I most wanted distance from.

The two police officers in charge of keeping an eye on us settled themselves in the attached suite while we did our best to make ourselves at home. The kitchen was well stocked, and they had set us up with a big-screen TV and free access to movies on demand. If it weren't for the fact we couldn't leave without putting our lives in danger, we could easily imagine ourselves to be on a restful vacation somewhere.

It was late evening. We had finished eating dinner—which I had insisted on cooking for fear of ending up with frozen fries and a hot dog—when I decided to call Dave. I still hadn't heard from him and I was beginning to worry.

To my great relief, he picked up after a couple rings. "Dave, thank God!" I exclaimed. Jem squirmed beside me on the couch. "I was getting worried."

"*You* were getting worried? Celia told me what happened. Are you okay?" His voice was frantic on the other end of the line.

At the sound of his warm voice I felt better. He was such a grounding element in my life; how could I even have considered betraying him? Shame invaded me and my cheeks burned. "We're doing fine, Dave."

There was a slight pause. "We…?"

Damn! Celia hadn't told him about Jem. What was wrong with my sister lately? Why wouldn't she have told him? What was that little twisted mind of hers up to now?

"Didn't Celia tell you? Jem was with me when we got kidnapped." That did not sound good at all. "I mean, we were kidnapped together."

"And he's there with you right now?" Dave did not sound like his usual happy-go-lucky self.

"Yes, he's here." Maybe if I spoke really softly he wouldn't hear it. Jem gave me a sly look as if he were enjoying the show. "It's not like I had a choice, Dave. The police told us we were in danger, and this was the only way they could protect us."

I heard a snort from the other end. How dare he?

"It wasn't like you were waiting by the phone anyway. No one could reach you for over a day. Where in heaven's name were you?" Whoa. Where was that coming from? Why was I mad at Dave? After all, he did have a good reason to be jealous and suspicious.

"I was at a job site with no phone signal and when I went to my motel for the night I realized I had left my charger at home," he said, confirming what I had already thought. "I'm sorry, Emily. I feel terrible that I wasn't there while this whole thing was going down, but I had no way of knowing...."

Guilt flooded my heart. "No, I'm sorry." My voice dropped an octave. "Of course you had no way of knowing. I'm just very tense, Dave." I had turned my back on Jem so he couldn't see me, but I could still feel the burn of his glare on my back.

"Of course you are, sweetheart. I'm being insensitive," Dave said. "You've been through a lot. As long as you're safe now, I don't care who's with you. I trust you." Oh boy, I really hoped that trust was deserved. "I'll let you go. Rest."

"I love you, Dave," I whispered, hoping Jem wouldn't hear me. But when I hung up and turned around, my eyes met his and I knew he wasn't happy.

"Boyfriend worried much?" he said, spitting the words like poison.

"What do you think? He loves me, after all."

My words were meant to hurt him, and they hit their mark. Jem's face dropped, and his jaw tensed up. "I won't bother you anymore. Good night." He got up and left me in the living room, alone and confused as usual.

My heart was bleeding. Hurting my best friend was like hurting myself. Sometimes it was almost like we were somehow connected; he hurt, I hurt. I hated him for making me feel at fault. Of all people, he had absolutely no right to make me feel like that.

Frustrated and angry, I searched for something to calm me down. A shower sounded great. A thorough scrubbing would be good for the soul as well. When I stood up, something fell from the couch to the floor. It was a wallet. Jem's wallet. It must have dropped from his pocket when he got up. It had fallen open on the floor and, when I bent down to pick it up, I noticed a picture inside—a picture of him and me during my Asian-exploration year. I was dressed in a red kimono, my black hair in a bob, my eyes heavily outlined in kohl to bring out their almond shape. Beside me, Jem, young and beautiful, had his arm over my shoulders and a big, generous smile on his lips. I remembered that day well. Then again, I remembered every day with Jem, no matter how much he had hurt me or how much he now annoyed me.

I put the picture back and left the wallet on top of the cocktail table. Forgetting about the shower, I opened the door to the bedroom and, before I was even aware of what I was doing, I was curled under the sheets and fast asleep.

I woke up suddenly, not sure how long I had slept. A soft groaning reached my ears, and I started. While my eyes adjusted to the dimness of the room, I realized the noise was coming from Jem. What was wrong with him?

I slid off my bed and approached his. "Jem. Are you okay?"

His eyes were closed, but he tossed and turned as if in pain. He was having a nightmare. "No, no. Please, don't...," he moaned.

I stood there, trying to decide what to do. Should I let him be, or should I wake him up from whatever night terror was assailing him? Watching him writhe in fear was painful. His face was contorted into a frown of agony. My stomach tightened.

Before I could stop myself, I sat down on the edge of his bed. I brushed his brow with my hand, trying to erase the worry and pain, and he calmed down, his muscles relaxing at my touch. God, he was so beautiful. An angel in his sleep. His muscled chest belied his boyish looks. I sighed. It was so hard being mad at him when he was right in front of me. From a distance, I was able to hate him and wish him all kinds of ungodly mishaps. In his presence, I was barely capable of doing much more than sticking my tongue out at him like a child.

"Em," he uttered, his eyes fluttering open. "Are you okay?"

I realized I had tears in my eyes. Grateful for the darkness, I pulled my hand away from his face. "I'm okay. You were a little agitated in your sleep."

He turned on his side, resting his head on his arm. "Bad dreams," he said. "I get them a lot. Nothing like being isolated from everyone you love to give you all kinds of nightmares."

I wiped my eyes and moved to stand, but Jem held my hand. "Stay with me. Like you used to."

I shook my head. "No, Jem. I can't. Not a good idea." A great lump grew in my throat.

He lifted his head. "No, I don't mean like that," he said. "Lie down with me for the night. I promise I won't do anything. I just need my best friend close."

Hesitant at first, I had to admit that I also needed a friendly body next to mine. I was still shaking inside from our misadventures and I did miss my best friend. So much, it hurt.

Jem flipped the edge of the covers off so I could slide beside him. "Jem, nothing can happen, do you understand? I know you don't want to believe me, but I love Dave."

"I understand," he told me, his eyes moist. "I don't like it, but I get it. I promise."

I stretched in bed, my back turned to him. His hand came over me and I felt his breath on my neck. "Good night, Emily Rose."

"Good night, Jem." His breathing quickly evened out and slowed. He was fast asleep.

In the morning, the sun woke me up as it sneaked in the room through a small gap in the curtains. I stretched and realized Jem still had his arm draped over me, his legs bent behind my back, cradling me against him. My heart grew wings. *I have to get up.* But it felt so right, it felt like home, and I couldn't make myself move away. I lay still, enjoying his heat, afraid of breaking the contact.

"You feel so good," he whispered in my ear, startling me off my semitrance. Instinctively I moved my body away from his. "Don't! Stay for a little while…."

I twisted myself around to look at him. "You promised me, Jeremy Peter." The accusation in my tone made him flinch. "Let me go."

He loosened his grip on me, and I slipped out of bed. "Party pooper," he muttered. "It's not like we have anywhere to go."

On my knees, I searched for my slippers and found them under his bed. "I don't know about you, but I'm hungry."

He perked up, his eyes opening wide. "Bacon and eggs?" he asked eagerly.

With a roll of my eyes, I slid my feet into the slippers and opened the door. "Oh hell. You and your junk food will be the death of me." I groaned at the idea. "All right, I'll make some bacon and eggs. Get up."

He shifted his legs over the side of the bed and sat up. "Hash browns?"

"Arghhh…." There was no way I was frying potatoes. The smell alone would clog my arteries. I stomped out of the room.

The sound of dragging feet was soon followed by his scuttling out of the room. His tousled hair stuck out every which way, and he had put his T-shirt on inside out. I giggled and opened the fridge.

"What's so funny?" He sat on a barstool and got busy peeling an orange.

"Never mind." I pulled a whole slab of bacon and the egg carton out of the fridge. "I can't believe you eat this crap all the time and stay fit."

"I haven't eaten good bacon in five years. The French may be famous for their cooking, but bacon is not their thing."

I dropped an egg, and its insides spread quickly across the counter. My eyes followed the flow of the egg white as my anger began a slow burn in my chest. Did he really just bring up France? "Thanks for reminding me that I'm still mad at you." It came out like a hiss.

Jem's head snapped up. "What? Shit. I'm sorry, Em. I didn't mean it that way." He jumped from his perch and ran around the counter to hold me by the arms. "Please, don't get mad again."

Anger boiling inside of me, I shrugged him off and walked away. "Make your own bacon!"

The air outside was chilly, and I immediately regretted not having grabbed my jacket. Still wearing my pj's, I knocked at the door of the attached suite to let the guards know I was going for a jog. One of them insisted on following me. I wish I could say I lost him easily, but I very rarely ran. In fact, I reserved running for emergencies—like if I were being chased by a bull or fleeing from a burning building. My jog quickly turned into a sluggish walk, and as my anger ebbed away so did my energy. At some point, I gave up and sat down on a tree stump.

"You are not a jogger, are you?" the policeman said, coming to a stop beside me.

I laughed. "What gave me away? The turtle-like progress or the floppy-arm action?"

"I've seen worse," he said, leaning against a tree trunk. "Mad?"

I nodded. It was getting very cold, sitting in the frigid air in my thin cotton pajamas. I rubbed my arms. "Very mad and very cold." I laughed again and hopped to my feet. "Better go in before I grow icicles on my nose."

The nice officer walked me back to the house. Obviously used to being a fly on the wall, he didn't say a word until we got to the front door. Courteously, he opened it and waited for me to go in. "Call me if you get mad again. I'll be glad to jog behind you. Maybe next time we can even break a sweat." He smiled.

"Thank you. I'm more of a yoga girl." I closed the door behind me.

Jem had set the small table by the window. An appetizing spread of bread, fruits, and poached eggs sat on the two plates. "I made breakfast," he said, unnecessarily. "No saturated fats. I couldn't find whole grain bread though. I hope white is okay. I toasted it…."

He had such a wistful expression on his face as he stood there, holding the back of a chair, that I smiled. I couldn't help it. My anger was gone and he looked positively so… Jem.

We sat and ate breakfast in silence. Surprisingly, the food was delicious. Jem had never been able to cook this well. His idea of a meal was a microwaved hot dog and a bag of chips. Finished with the last of the fruit, I wiped my lips on the napkin and stole a glance toward him.

"Listen, Em," he said, serious and contrite. "I know France is a sore spot for us, but like it or not, it's part of my life and it will creep up every so often. You can't get mad at me every time I mention something that happened while I was there. I can't erase the last few years—as much as I would like to."

He was right, of course. However, I didn't have much control over my feelings when it came to him. "I'll try. I can't promise though. It's still all very fresh," I said. "Give me time."

"You can have all the time you need." Jem covered my hand with his. "Just don't take too long." He smiled that brilliant smile of his, and I had to laugh.

***

"Did you like it?" my sister asked at the other end of the line.

"Oh my gosh, Celia! Thank you so much." I was still going through the contents of the care package Celia had sent us. So many little treasures in it. "How did you know I wanted to read *Cinder*?"

My crazy sister laughed. "I hacked into your Goodreads account. Hell, you have an impressive list of books to read." It was true. I did have an enormous list of books I wanted to read sometime in the future. It spanned many genres and age groups.

"Tell her thanks for the Oreos and crackers," Jem yelled from the kitchen, where he was busy putting away the junk food my sister had sent him. "Oh yeah. Tell her the chocolate-covered chips were a stroke of genius."

In another world, another life, my sister and Jem would

have made the perfect match. I smiled. "Did you hear that, Celia?"

"Tell him I will send him a couple boxes of frozen White Castle sliders next time," she said.

Jem, finished stocking the kitchen shelves with every bit of bad-for-you food known to mankind, sat beside me on the couch and curiously looked through the stuff my sis had sent me. "What the hell is this?" he asked, holding a small backpack up.

"That's my emergency bag. Thank you, sis, for remembering to send it, by the way," I said to both Jem and Celia. "In that bag I have anything and everything I need to survive for a week under any condition."

"Yep, my always prepared sister," Celia yelled.

Jem had unzipped the bag and was removing items from it. "Foil blankets, hand warmers, dehydrated food… toilet paper?" He was holding up a roll with a quizzical look. "You really haven't changed, Em."

I grabbed the toilet paper out of his hands. "Better prepared than sorry," I recited.

A familiar refrain for anyone who had known me since my childhood. I felt safe if I knew I was prepared for any eventuality. When I was in college my friends knew they could come to me anytime they had a headache or needed a tampon. I always carried a giant purse stocked with things I would most likely never need.

"Marcy wanted me to ask you if you used the potion she gave you," Celia stated, while I retrieved my emergency items from Jem's hands.

"No need," I said. "Everything's okay. Have you seen Dave?"

My sister was quiet for a moment. "Yes, he… is worried about you." She was hiding something. I could always tell by the way her voice became just a little higher than usual.

"Celia, what's going on? I can tell something is up." I said. "Is he sick?"

"There's nothing wrong. Really." There was definitely something wrong. "Did Detective Jarvas tell you when you guys can expect this whole thing to be over?"

Nice deflective move. "He seems to think one more week or so," I told her, willingly letting go of the issue—whatever it might have been.

"Good. You need to come home." And there it was again. That note of urgency and concern.

After the phone call, I went out to the porch to read the book my sister had sent me. Jem was fiddling with the television set, and I needed quiet for a few moments. The tone I heard in my sister's voice after I had mentioned Dave really worried me. What exactly could be wrong? I realized that I was probably being a little too paranoid due to our recent misadventures, and I allowed myself to dive headfirst into the novel in my hands.

My concentration was broken when a loud noise came from inside the house, closely followed by a cry of pain. My legs reacted before I even knew what was happening. I jumped off my seat and ran indoors, where I found Jem on the floor of the kitchen, hugging his leg.

"What happened?" The two officers had also run to check

on the commotion. "Are you hurt?"

A string of curses flew out of Jem's mouth. He really must be hurting. Jem rarely cursed. One of his many idiosyncrasies, and one I was particularly fond of.

"I twisted my freaking ankle," he said.

One of the cops immediately went to the freezer for a bag of ice. The other crouched beside Jem and asked, "Do we need to call for medical attention?"

I knelt by Jem and, lifting the bottom of his pants, I examined his ankle. It was swollen, but did not feel like it was broken. "Let's put some ice on it and wait a while to see if it helps," I told the officer. "How in heaven's name did you manage to do this, Jem?" I applied the bag of ice the other policeman handed to me.

"I was getting the Oreos from the cabinet and I stepped and slipped on something." Jem closed his eyes in pain as the sting of the ice hit the skin on his bruised ankle. "Ouch. Are you sure it's not broken?"

I felt around his ankle again. "I don't think so. Try to move it." He moved it easily. "No, not broken. Come on, let's sit you down and put that foot up."

With the help of one of the officers, I was able to guide Jem to the couch, where I propped his leg on a big cushion. "You will do just about anything for attention, won't you?"

He snorted and threw me a mischievous look. "Did it work?"

I squeezed his ankle and he yelped. "You're pitiful." I walked away to go pour him a glass of water.

"Is he going to be all right?" my jogging companion asked.

"He'll be fine," I said. "Thank you for helping. I'll call you if we need you."

From my position in the kitchen I could watch Jem unnoticed. Being immobilized did not agree with him. I remember another time—we were still kids—when he had broken a leg. The first few days had been hell. Jem's refusal to be still for very long had earned him an emergency surgery then. I hoped his ankle would heal quickly, or he would drive me insane.

My sister had sent a small box of old pictures in her care package and I decided that would be a good distraction. I grabbed it out of the box I had stored in my room and returned to the living room to sit by him.

"Scoot," I said, shoving his legs out of the way and being rewarded with a groan of pain.

"Ouch! Easy, girly." He gingerly propped himself up a bit more and opened a space for me to sit. "You're having way too much fun hurting me."

I smirked like the Cheshire cat and removed the lid of the box.

"Are you up for a stroll down memory lane?" He looked up at me, a question in his eyes. "Sis sent a bunch of old pictures for us to reminisce over. I have a sneaky suspicion she's up to something." *And I know exactly what it is, but I am not about to tell you.*

"I love pictures." I knew he did.

When we were kids we would spend an inordinate amount of time staring and commenting on pictures from when we were babies or when our parents were kids themselves. His eyes would become unfocused and he would slouch on the couch or wherever we were at the time, ready to indulge in the past. He would then relish in telling and retelling—often many times over—stories he had heard from our parents or from each other. Even as a young girl, I used to love watching how animated he would suddenly become, his hands moving around like those of a maestro conducting his orchestra—except there were no instruments, only memories.

I handed him the box and he buried his hands inside, as if hungry for whatever comfort those pictures brought him. Pain obviously forgotten, he pulled a picture out of the box and waved it at me.

"Look. This is when we went on that trip to the beach. How old were we?"

I took a peek at the photograph and smiled. "Fourteen, we were fourteen." The memories came flooding back. "You had turned fourteen that summer and I was about to have my birthday in early fall."

Jem laughed, a happy, genuine belly chuckle that shook the whole couch and made me smile wider. "I remember you getting super jealous because I was paying attention to all these girls." He pointed at the blurred figures of a couple young girls in the background.

I feigned outrage. "I was not jealous. I was annoyed that we were together on vacation and my best friend paid more attention to two strange girls than me." The memory of red-hot jealousy came to me as fresh as if it were happening right then.

With a shrug, Jem threw the photo in the box. "What did

you expect from a teenage boy? My hormones were raging and I had very little control over them."

I frowned. "So, I guess not much has changed, then."

It was meant as a joke, but Jem swallowed hard and shook his head slowly. "I'm not controlled by my hormones anymore, Emily Rose."

Better to pretend I didn't hear the hurt in his voice.

"Whatever!" I bent forward and took another picture from the box, hoping to defuse the awkwardness. "This is a good one." I couldn't help but laugh. That photo documented one of the funniest moments in our past. I handed it to him.

The reaction was immediate. "Oh shit! I thought we had burned this one."

Back then, Jem thought he would show his support for my ethnic/cultural quest by dressing up in traditional Japanese clothes. Not only did he look ridiculous in that flowery kimono, but he had decided that a fake mustache would give him so much more credibility as an older Japanese man. The mustache, a fuzzy, black thing that drooped from his upper lip to his chin, made him look like a comical Confucius. I had taken the picture back then and told him I would keep it so I could blackmail him with it anytime I wanted something from him.

Tears were rolling out of our eyes, and our laughter seemed to swell and continue forever, fed by renewed glances at the photograph. It finally exhausted itself.

"Young people can be so goofy," I said, willing to generalize Jem's extreme silliness when I fully knew there were few as silly as he had been as a young man.

Jem had pulled another picture out of the box and was staring at it, head cocked to the side and a dreamy expression in his eyes. "Wow!" he exclaimed, still staring at the photo in wonder. "I forgot how absolutely gorgeous you were when we were in college."

My heart thumped in my chest, as if trying to get out. "What?" What was he up to now? Would he ever stop trying to win me over to his side?

He sighed and handed me the picture. It was a photograph someone had taken of me—was it Jem?—during my senior year in college. While everyone had gone on spring break to the beach, I had decided to go on a yoga retreat. There I was, in my yoga pants, my black, slick hair—the longest I ever had it—pouring down all the way to my waist, and a skintight top. My cheeks burned. I had never thought of myself as gorgeous. It was strange to look at my younger self through Jem's eyes.

"Stop blushing like you didn't know you were a freaking hot babe," Jem said, a little smile on his lips.

I didn't. I really didn't.

"Stop messing with me, Jeremy Peter. It's not nice to mock an old friend."

Jem tried to move his foot so he could scoot closer, and he flinched in renewed pain. "You're kidding me, right?" he said instead. "All my friends begged me to get you to consider them as your dates."

My mouth fell open. "You never told me that."

"That's because I didn't want any of those jokers to go out with you. Ever." His voice was quiet and serious, all the joking gone from him.

"Why not?" The question came out unbidden.

"Because, Emily Rose, I was so freaking in love with you I couldn't bear even the thought of another guy looking at you, much less taking you out." I had reached out and handed him the photograph. His fingers lingered on mine a little too long, setting my skin on fire.

I dropped my gaze to my lap and played with my hands. *Damn you, Jem! Back to awkward.*

"I'm going to get something to drink. Do you want something?"

He had no time to answer my question. I jumped to my feet and almost ran to hide in the kitchen. As I turned on the lights, I wondered why it was so dark in there. It was only late morning and it had been sunny just a little bit ago. The window behind the sink was wet and I realized it was raining. Not only raining, it seemed. The wind buffeted the trees outside, forcing them into a frenzied dance, and the sun had been hidden by thick, rolling, ominous clouds that raced through the skies.

As I was turning around to go back to Jem, one of the officers poked his head in. "There's a big storm brewing," he said. "Be prepared."

Be prepared? How do you prepare for a storm that's already upon you? There was no basement, we were in the middle of the woods with the high possibility of flying branches and falling trees, and Jem could barely walk.

"Stay away from the windows," the policeman said before closing the door.

Away from the windows? There were windows in every

room of that house.

I walked to the adjoining door and knocked. "Excuse me, Officer," I said. "There are windows in every room."

"The storage room," the man said. "Get in there to weather the storm. We're monitoring it and we'll let you know if something else happens."

Jem was staring out the window at the angry wind howling and hissing. "Shit! What do we do?"

A loud, scary thunderclap shook the whole cabin, and I ducked as if lightning had hit me. "We go into the storage room. Come on."

After I had placed Jem safe and sound inside the small storage, I came back to the couch to grab some pillows, a blanket, and my emergency bag. At the last minute, I decided to grab the box of photographs as well. What if a window broke and the rain soaked the interior of the living room? We would lose all those memories.

I propped Jem's leg on a pillow and then sat on the floor next to him, leaning on the other. "Are you cold?" I asked, showing him the blanket.

He grabbed the blanket from my hands and grinned. "You're not my mom, Emily Rose. I'm not a baby anymore, you know?"

God, did I know!

"Just making sure you don't die on my watch," I said, trying to defuse the tightness in my gut with a joke.

I settled myself down, fluffing the cushion behind me. The light inside the storage was dim and made everything look gloomy and blurry. I pulled out my book, but I had a sneaky suspicion I wouldn't be able to read in this light.

A loud thunderclap echoed through the house, shaking everything. A few items, hanging precariously on the shelves above us, fell, and I jumped.

"Are you okay?" Jem asked, looking at me worried. He knew well how storms, especially those involving a lot of wind, made me very nervous. One time my mom and dad had taken us on a vacation to the Caribbean. An awful hurricane had rolled over the island a few days after we had arrived. I had never been able to look at wind the same way again.

"I'm fine," I said, even though inside I was shaking a little. The booms of the thunder and the sound of the wind, like a banshee on the loose, were making me a bit jumpy.

Jem's face opened up in a smile. "Do you remember that storm when we were in fifth grade?" I shook my head, thinking but coming up empty. "Yes, you do. We were being dismissed from school and as we were running to the bus, a cloud opened up and we were drenched before we could get to the bus."

"I do remember." A memory flashed in my head. "We were so soaked we left a puddle on the floor of the bus."

"And you kept complaining about your hair—"

"Because I had just spent a ton of money on a hairdo at a fancy hairstylist," I finished.

We laughed in unison. Until another clap of thunder made me jump again. I was shivering in earnest now.

Jem waved his hand, calling me to his side. "Come closer," he said. "Come on. You're shaking like Jell-O in an earthquake."

"Nice. Comparing me to food," I protested. But I did switch sides, coming to sit right next to him.

He spread the blanket over my legs and pulled me against him. "Just because we're at odds doesn't mean we're not friends still."

Hesitantly at first, I allowed him to pull my head onto his shoulder in the protective move he had always resorted to when I was scared or hurt. It felt safe in his arms, even after all that had happened.

"I didn't live with her," Jem said, his quiet voice breaking the moment of silence.

"With who?" I asked, knowing all too well who he was talking about.

"Tina. I never lived with her." His other hand had crawled over the blanket to grip mine. "Not here and not in France. We got separate apartments. In fact, after the first year we didn't even see each other that often."

"Why are you telling me this?" I didn't dare look at him.

"Because I want you to know that it was never about Tina—or sex with Tina. It was always about putting some space between us, to stop me from making a fool out of myself and destroying the best thing in my life."

"How can you be so sure it would destroy our friendship?" I asked, my head stubbornly lowered.

"I can't, but I was so afraid…. You were my best friend, Emily Rose, and I couldn't risk it." Silence fell over us, interrupted every so often by the rumble of thunder and the screeching of the wind.

Finally, unable to contain myself any longer, I whispered,

"If you had asked me out I would have said yes."

I felt him shudder, and my heart clenched—for him and for me. Five years of wasted time, of heartbreak and doubt, had passed, and there was no going back. My eyesight got blurry, and I wiped the tears away with the back of my hand. Jem squeezed me closer and brushed a hand over my head in a gentle, comforting caress.

My anger at him had been finally replaced by a deep sadness. *Is it possible to miss something you never had?*

Chapter Eight

Pain and Hope

"I'm telling you, you need to get out of there right now." Marcy's voice came through strident and panicky.

What have I done to be surrounded by crazy people?

"Marcy, calm down," I told her, drawing little circles in the air by my temple. Jem laughed. "Everything is fine. We are perfectly safe here."

I heard her inhale sharply and then let out a big sigh. "I had a premonition this morning," she said. "There is a very ugly aura color over you guys right now. Bad news."

My attempt at sounding patient was not going well. "You don't even know where we are," I said. Hell, I barely knew where we were myself! "How can you see this aura?"

I heard Marcy utter an expletive, followed by whispers in the background. "I saw it in my vision this morning. Both you and Jem were surrounded by this nasty puke-colored aura."

I choked. "Are you sure it wasn't more like a pus-colored

one?" Okay. Maybe it wasn't very nice of me to mock my sweet, yet oh-so-crazy witch friend, but I couldn't resist it.

"Don't laugh," she chided. "No joking matter. You and Jem are in serious danger. You have to talk to Detective Jarvas and have him relocate you."

My sister's voice replaced Marcy's. "Do what Marcy says," she screamed. I pulled the phone away from my aching ear. "Don't be stupid. Marcy's premonitions always come true."

Now I was annoyed and had a ringing in my ear. "You mean, like the potion that was supposed to keep Jem away from me?"

Crap! I had forgotten he was right there, just a few feet away. His head snapped up. He didn't say anything, but I could almost read the question in his eyes. I turned my back on him, determined not to let him see me sweat.

"Must I remind you that the potion actually worked?" My sister's voice had acquired the usual petulant tone she often used with me when she thought I was being unreasonable. "*You* are the one who lied about not loving him."

"Be that as it may, I couldn't even tell you where I am so I'm pretty sure we are in no danger here. Aura or no aura." I'd had it with the conversation. I said my good-byes and hung up.

Jem looked up from the book he was reading. "What are the crazies going on about now?" he asked with a grin.

"Apparently our auras are having a color crisis." I dropped into one of the overstuffed armchairs.

"What?" Jem's eyebrows shot up.

I waved my hand up in the air, picked up the remote, and

turned on the TV. "Never mind. Crazy stuff."

He was quiet for a minute. "You bought a potion to keep me away from you?"

I closed my eyes and turned my head up to the ceiling. "Oh my God! What is wrong with you guys today?" I jumped off the couch and went to hide in the bedroom.

I must have fallen asleep, because I was woken by a loud popping noise coming from outside, soon followed by a crashing sound. I ran out to the living room just in time to see Jem being grabbed by two strange men in camo uniforms and masks.

My limbs froze for a moment as my brain tried to process what I was witnessing. One man had Jem in a headlock and was dragging him out the door. The other was coming toward me, a gun pointed at my chest.

I turned to run but it was too late. In a few strides, the masked man had caught me in a tight grip. Struggling didn't seem to have any effect on him, as his hold tightened around me while he pulled me outdoors. In a moment of lucidity, I wondered where our watchmen were. Then I saw them—their bodies lying in a puddle of blood right inside the door to their suite.

I struggled harder. It didn't make a difference. This guy had muscles that would make the Rock look weak. God knew my wimpy muscles were no match for his. He had me packed into the trunk of their car in no time, not even bothering to tie me up. Jem was already there, lying curled up on his side, unmoving.

"Jem," I called once the trunk had been closed and the only

light was coming from a couple holes in the back. Jem didn't answer. "Jem, what's wrong?"

I felt around, shaking him and looking for signs of life, but couldn't find any. My heart was racing and tears rolled down my face. "Jem, please be okay."

Images of the cops, injured or dead as we left the area, haunted me. I shook Jem again. Fear filled my heart and I started hyperventilating. Fraught with anxiety and having trouble breathing in the confined space, I slowly felt myself drift into the oblivion of unconsciousness.

***

Coming to was not pleasant. My whole body was cramped from being curled up for so long—or so I assumed. I really couldn't be sure since I had passed out pretty early on. I was not in the trunk anymore. It was a small room with concrete floors and not much more. Light filtered through a very dirty, very small window up high on the wall, and an even smaller one on the door. A bunk of sorts hung from one of the walls and something that looked an awful lot like a toilet adorned the corner. With a jolt, I realized it was indeed a toilet. Was I in a prison cell?

"Jem!" The memory hit me like a ton of bricks. Still finding it hard to move, I looked around me for the familiar figure of my best friend, but no luck. He hadn't been moving in the car. In fact, I had not been able to feel a heartbeat. Was he…?

No! No! I couldn't even wrap my head around that possibility. He was fine. He had to be. I had lost him once already. The idea of losing him again was unbearable.

I checked myself to see if I had a phone on me, but no such luck this time. I had left the burner phone on the living room table. *Stupid!*

My legs refused to hold me for long, so I sat on the edge of the bunk to catch my breath and clear my head. I couldn't think straight as pictures of a dead Jem clouded my head. My eyes burned with tears and I hung my head, feeling lonely and hopeless.

A noise snapped me out of my funk. The door opened halfway with a great screech of rusty hinges, and a body was unceremoniously thrown in through the gap. I jumped to my feet and ran to him as the door closed again.

It was Jem. I fell to my knees, ignoring the sharp pain in my joints. "Jem!" I yelled, throwing myself across his prostrate body. Much to my relief, he moved under me.

I gently turned him around so I could look at him, and I choked up a sob. My heart stopped. His face was a mottled red and purple. His gorgeous blue eyes were so swollen I doubted he could see anything through them, and his lip was busted and bleeding. I shook him gently, afraid to cause him any more pain, but wanting him awake and alert.

A soft moan came out of his ruptured lips, and my heart began beating again. "What did they do to you?"

"Em," he managed to say, lifting his hand to touch my face. "Are you okay?"

With tears rolling freely and profusely down my cheeks, I nodded, and held his hand against my face. "I'm fine. What happened? You look awful."

In spite of the terrible injuries to his face, he laughed softly. "Painfully honest, as usual."

I giggled through my quiet sobs. "I didn't mean it that way." I touched his face, checking his wounds. "They did a number on you."

"That's only what you can see," he said. *Shit! I didn't even think about that.* He probably had more injuries under his clothes.

Frantically, I began pulling on the edges of his T-shirt, trying to look at his skin underneath. "Whoa, girl. I don't think I'm up to that right now," he joked. My heart melted all over again. Stupid, sweet, tougher-than-he-looked Jem.

Feeling the urge to hug him, I examined his belly and torso and cringed. He had huge bruises stretching across his abdomen and chest. When I touched the angry wound covering his stomach, he flinched. "You may have some internal bleeding, Jem."

For a second, I wished my sister was there with her medical knowledge and experience. *Scratch that.* If she were there she would also be in danger. I and my very limited medical skills would have to do. "Let's try to put you up on the bunk." I slid his arm over my shoulder to try and pull him up to his feet. He groaned in pain but slowly stood up, holding on to his stomach. "Just a few more steps, Jem. You can do it."

Once I had him lying on the narrow bunk, I pulled his shirt over his head and looked around for a container of any kind. Close to the toilet and the tiny sink, there were a couple plastic cups and a towel. Keeping my eye on Jem, I filled one of the cups and dipped the corner of the towel in water.

"I'm going to try and clean your wounds a bit, Jem," I told him, studying the blood-covered injuries on his face and stomach. "It will hurt."

Jem held back the screams from the pain he was undoubtedly feeling while I ministered to him. In place of ice, I drenched the towel in the very cold water from the faucet and placed it on top of the worst bruises, hoping it would bring some of the swelling down. There was no way of knowing what was going on beneath his skin, and I hoped to God he wasn't bleeding inside.

Once he was as cleaned as I could manage with the resources I had, I stretched out alongside him, my head gingerly lying on his shoulder. "Is this okay? Does it hurt?" I asked, lifting my head slightly to look at him. I couldn't tell whether his eyes were open or closed.

"It feels heavenly," he whispered, his hand coming to rest on the arm I had draped across his chest. "I think I probably died and went to heaven."

"Don't joke around," I said, sobbing anew. "You're seriously hurt."

He caressed my arm. "I'm not joking." His voice came out labored. *I hope his lungs are okay.* "But seriously. Do I have to get beaten within an inch of death for you to touch me like this?"

I buried my face into the crook of his neck and cried in earnest, my sobs shaking him as much as they shook me. "Sorry, Jem. I—"

His hand went to my head, and his swollen lips brushed my forehead. "Don't cry," he whispered. "I'll be fine. The scars will make me look sexier."

On that note, I think we both fell asleep, physically and mentally exhausted.

When I woke up, it was dark in the room. What looked like an emergency light on the wall had lit up and was shedding a sickly glow into the utterly depressing space.

I lifted my head slowly, afraid to wake up Jem, but he was already awake. "Did you sleep at all?" I asked, worried.

"I did," he said. In the semidarkness, his bruises looked even gloomier. "I was watching you sleep. You looked like an angel."

My heart fluttered a little. Lifting myself on one arm to better look at him, I giggled. "Flattery will not get you anything from this girl." I tried to slide out of the bunk without moving him. "Are you in pain?"

He nodded. "A little," he lied, the mere effort of moving his head making him flinch. "Do you think I could have some water?"

When I came back with a cup of water, he had managed to sit up on the bunk, supported by the wall. He took the cup to his lips and drank it all in one go. He was so bruised it hurt me just looking at him.

"Why did they do that to you?" I asked, taking the cup away from him.

"Tina," he replied, wiping his lips with the back of his hand. "They're still under the impression I know where she is. They beat me up to get the information out of me."

I sucked in a gulp of air. "What stopped them?" Had Jem given them any information at all?

"I think they wanted to be sure I was still alive," he said with a chuckle. "You know, so I can handle another round of torture later."

My legs buckled under me, and I had to grab hold of the wall in order not to fall. "You think they're going to do this again?" An uncontrollable tremor started making its way up my legs. "Why won't they believe that you know nothing?"

"Five years on the lam with Tina," he muttered. "They think we were an item and that there's no way she didn't tell me. They'll come for me again." His voice trembled. "They may come for you, too, Emily Rose."

It was too much. I sat down on the edge of the bunk, shaking as if an earthquake was ripping me apart. "They'll kill you."

"They'll kill me regardless," he said matter-of-factly. "They also think I know what Tina saw, and that I can be used as a witness against them. As soon as I've served my purpose, they'll kill me."

Forgetting his injuries, I practically threw myself in his arms. "No, Jem, I won't let them!"

"I'm worried about you," he said, his lips close to my ear. "I got myself in this mess. You just had the misfortune of knowing me."

My face was only a few inches away from his, and I could just see the glint of his ocean-blue eyes peeking through the swollen tissue. How I loved getting lost in those eyes! Even as kids, I would catch myself staring into his eyes and wondering what it would be like to lose myself in that expanse of blueness. Not much had changed. I still felt butterflies in my stomach and a burning in my lower abdomen every time I looked into them.

"I missed you." The admission came out of my mouth before I could stop it. It was true, of course. But it didn't mean I wanted him to know it. I also didn't want to do what I did next.

I kissed him. Full frontal, lip-to-lip kiss.

He winced but then relaxed into the kiss, his arms tightening around me. He tasted like blood, and I remembered how badly his lips had been hurt. With a gentle tug, I pulled away from him.

A moan escaped his lips, and I wasn't quite sure if it was from pain or disappointment. "You had to pick a time when I'm a walking wound to kiss me," he joked.

Shame and guilt took over. "I shouldn't have done that," I said, flustered. "I'm sorry. I don't know why I did that."

He grabbed my hand in his. "I'm not complaining and I'm not asking why," he said. "I'm just happy you did it."

As I slid off the bunk and my feet hit the concrete floor, I felt dizzy, as if all the revelations of the last few hours were too overwhelming for me. "What do we do?" I asked, pacing the floor. "What can we do?"

Jem's breath came out a bit wheezy, and I worried again that his lungs had been compromised during the beating.

"I don't know," he confessed. "Short of knocking them out senseless—which we won't be able to do—I have no clue what to do next."

Those words brought a foggy memory to mind. My hand went to my neck where a little red bottle was hanging from a chain. "How many men are there total?" I asked, the kernel of an idea taking seed in my brain.

"I saw only two," Jem said. "But they're built like freaking rocks. Trust me. I tried to fight them."

"Do you think we could take one?" Two against one. It could be done, right?

It was hard to decipher any expression in Jem's face right now, but I guessed he was looking at me with suspicion. "I guess we could. Why?"

I squeezed the red vial a little tighter. "I have an idea."

***

With a sketch of a plan made, we were both able to rest a little. We slept in spurts, followed by periods of total alertness during which we reviewed our plan, trying to convince ourselves it would work. It *had* to work!

Whenever Jem was sleeping and I was awake, I watched him with growing concern as his breathing became more labored and sounds of crackling echoed in his chest. Something inside his lungs was not right, and I could only hope and pray it was nothing terribly serious. The thought of losing him was as unbearable as the thought of losing a limb or my heart.

Morning found us wide-awake, Jem lying flat on his back and I stretched beside him, my head on his chest listening for his heartbeat, as if to assure myself he was still alive and well. My stomach grumbled with hunger and my bladder begged to be emptied. I hadn't used the toilet once since we had been brought there, and even my teacher's bladder couldn't hold it that long.

"I have to use the toilet," I said, my demanding bladder winning over my embarrassment. "Can you look the other way? Please?"

With considerable trouble, he turned to the wall, offering me the privacy I needed to relieve myself. I didn't remember ever having gone in front of anyone other than my sister, and that's when we were kids. I was mortified.

"This definitely takes our relationship to a whole new level," Jem said, his back toward me. "Sharing a bathroom moment puts us level with married couples."

Annoying man! "Stop, Jem. This is embarrassing enough as it is. Talking through it does not make it better."

"Emily Rose, we've known each other since preschool." His voice reflected surprise.

"That doesn't mean I want to share my private… moments with you." I hated to sound so whiny, but this was too much.

Jem laughed. "For God's sake, Em! Everybody pees. It's not a big deal," he said.

I flushed and gave a silent thank-you that they had left us some toilet paper. "Well, it is for me. You can turn around."

While I rinsed my hands in the sink, Jem slowly sat up. From the corner of my eye, I watched him stretching his muscles and wincing in pain with each move. I hadn't checked his legs. "Did they hit your legs, too?" I asked.

"Nothing terrible. A kick here and there." He sounded nonchalant and I knew he was doing that for my benefit. When he stood up I noticed how he favored the left leg and I knew something was wrong. Added to his earlier sprain, another leg injury would complicate things if we succeeded in fleeing this place.

"You should let me see that." I pointed at his leg. He was about to deny it. "I'm not arguing. Let me see it."

"Bossy as usual," he said under his breath. "Can I pee first?"

Heat rose to my cheeks and I turned my back on him. "You should have told me about your leg."

"The pain in my chest made me forget it," he said, flushing. "It's nothing. Just sore and a bit stiff."

He had walked to the edge of the bed where I was standing. With a big theatrical sigh, he pulled down his pants just enough to show me the alarming bruise on his right thigh.

"Hell, Jem," I exclaimed in shock. "We have to get out of here and take you to a hospital."

He looked at me through the slits that served as his eyes and chuckled. "You've got me with my pants down and that's all you can say?"

He was seized by a fit of coughing, and I couldn't hold it anymore—I cried, again. Jem hastily pulled his pants up and took a step to hold me against him.

"I'm okay, Emily Rose. Really," he whispered in my ear. "Do you remember that time when we were about fifteen and I fell off a moving bus?"

Did I ever! We were coming back from our first concert together and were late catching our bus home. When we got to the stop, the bus was already leaving. In a panic, we both ran and jumped inside. Except Jem lost his balance and rolled off the moving bus into the gravel road. By the time I managed to get the bus driver to stop, Jem was lying in the middle of the road, a bloody mess.

"You scared the crap out of me back then, too." I had no energy to sound flippant. I hid my wet face in his T-shirt and smelled blood.

"The point is that it looked a lot worse than it was." His hand cradled the back of my head. "When we got to the hospital, they cleaned all the scratches and gashes, and sent me home with antibiotic cream and some bandages. I was fine then and I will be fine now."

He rocked me gently and began to sing a familiar tune. I recognized the words and melody from an old favorite of mine.

I laughed and cried at the same time. "How do you remember that? I'm Kate Bush's biggest fan and I had almost forgotten that song. 'Rubberband Girl.'" The memory of all the times I had listened to and sung that song just to annoy him came flooding back, and an overwhelming sense of nostalgia took over.

A quiet laugh reached my ears. "Please, how could I forget it? You in a red wig, fake microphone in hand, singing your heart out…. No way will I ever forget it."

"I called myself the Asian Kate." I was laughing out loud now, momentarily forgetting where we were. Jem had always had the gift to make me forget hard times and bring a smile to my lips. I pushed myself apart from him just enough that I could look him in the eye. "I'm sorry, Jem, for all the nasty things I've said to you these past weeks. I was very angry."

He brushed a hand over my face. "I know. You had a right to be," he said. It was so hard to see his beautiful face so damaged. "I'm the one who's sorry, Emily Rose. Sorry for being a fool. Sorry for having left you without a good-bye. Sorry for putting you in this much danger."

We stared at each other silently for a moment. My heart was exploding out of my chest. There were so many things I was dying to say to him—words I had kept inside for so long they had grown roots inside my heart and soul. Words that if freed would, like a river, carve the geography of our future. I thought it better to keep them unsaid—for now, at least.

"Are you sure you can do this?" I asked him, worried about his strength.

"I distract one of them, you allow yourself to be caught by the other, knock him out, and then we both take the first one down." I laughed. He made it sound like a fight scene from an old movie. "Did I get it wrong?"

"No… you just made it sound like I'm going to punch the daylight out of him." When in fact the plan was to get him to take a whiff of Marcy's potion.

"Semantics—" His head popped up as the sound of a key turning in the door reached us loud and clear. "They're here!"

A shiver went through me. The time had come.

Chapter Nine

ESCAPE AND RESCUE

One advantage of doing yoga was the fact that I could bend my arms and legs in ways most people couldn't. As we waited for the two burly men to make their way into the room, my heart beating so loudly I could barely hear anything else, I bent my arm all the way behind my back. The silver chain holding the little red vial was hanging over my back, and I had wrapped my fingers around it, waiting for the right occasion to tear it off my neck.

Jem was next to me, holding on to the wall for dear life. His breathing was made worse by the anxiety of what was about to happen. We had one chance, and with Jem hurt and my lack of muscle strength, it was not a terribly bright one.

The door clanked open and the same two guys who had taken us from the cabin walked in. First thing I noticed was they carried no guns. At least not visibly. I was pretty sure they had one somewhere hidden. They knew our strength was no match for theirs. I gulped, suddenly very aware of how foolhardy our plan really was. We had to try though.

The biggest one went straight to Jem, hands up. I watched as my best friend flinched in fear and my heart just burst. No way! They were not going to hurt him again.

The second one was slower, probably relaxed in the knowledge that I was just a skinny, tiny Asian woman with no muscle and no girth to give him any trouble. "All right, lady," he rumbled. "No funny business and I won't hurt you… much." He laughed as if he had just told the funniest story in the world.

His companion, now holding a struggling Jem, also laughed. "This one already went one round," he said. "Round two is up."

The thug reached out and pulled me to him. As his arms went around to hold me against him, and before he could turn me around, I pulled on the chain and broke it. I brought my hand forward just as he roughly twirled me around to face him. I wasted no time. With my teeth, I uncorked the bottle and brought it quickly up close to his nose. Surprised, he first opened his eyes wide, then laughed, obviously unaffected by the potion.

I shoved the bottle closer to his nose. "What's that? It smells good," he said, laughing. Unfortunately for him, he also took a deep whiff of the sweet-smelling potion, and I watched as his eyes rolled back in his eye sockets. His trunk-like arms went slack and his body slid to the floor in a slow-motion movement that left me frozen for a moment or two. I held my breath for fear of inhaling it. That was some powerful stuff!

With no time to waste, I jumped at the other guy, who now had Jem in a headlock and, for lack of anything better, kicked him hard on the shins. He buckled a little and loosened his hold on Jem for a moment. Taking advantage, I stuck the bottle under the giant's nose while Jem took a knee to the man's privates.

We didn't stick around to see what happened next. I grabbed Jem's hand and pulled him along with me out the door, closing it behind me. "Run, Jem, run," I yelled before taking off as fast as my legs could carry me. Unfortunately, Jem couldn't move very fast, and I soon had to slow down so he could catch up with me.

I looked around us for the first time. We were in the middle of a huge walled courtyard. The high walls were topped with barbed wire and crumbling. The red-brick buildings had no windows other than tiny little slits spaced out evenly, and a couple guard towers flanked the yard. We were in an abandoned prison somewhere. The gate had been broken a long time ago and it stood wide open like the gaping mouth of a toothless monster. On the other side there was a forest—a thick wall of trees as far as the eye could see.

I took a quick glance behind us. We were not being followed. Yet. "We've got to move fast before they come after us," I said urgently.

Jem was not doing well. His leg injury, added to his twisted ankle, made him drag his leg rather than walk on it. I stopped and draped one of his arms over my shoulders. "I'm heavy," he protested. "I'll slow you down."

"If you think I'm going to leave you behind, you are even

dumber than you look," I said, supporting him and resuming our labored walk into the bowels of the forest. I looked at the looming evergreens with apprehension. Would we be able to find our way out? Following the road would be easier, but the odds the guys back in the cell would catch us were also a lot higher. Sticking to the woods was a calculated risk.

I lost track of time after the first half hour or so. Jem's crackling breath was a constant worry, and he was becoming heavier and heavier on my shoulder as his strength steadily waned. I knew he needed to rest, but I was afraid we were still too close to the prison to be able to breathe easy. I pushed on, in spite of my many misgivings.

To his credit, Jem did not complain once. He had to be in considerable pain, but he didn't utter a word. "We'll stop soon," I promised, looking behind us. There was no sign of anybody.

"Don't worry about me," he mumbled, his voice a little slurred. "I'm fine."

He was not fine. Underneath all the bruises, he had gone paler than a ghost, and I could feel his body shuddering out of control. I had to get him to safety fast.

After a while I felt a little more comfortable allowing us a few breaks to catch our breaths, but they were short and far in between. We were both thirsty and at one point, ignoring the risks, we drank from a puddle on the forest floor. God only knew how much bacteria and germs we ingested.

Jem had gone quieter as the day went on. By the time evening was falling, and with it the darkness of twilight, he had stopped talking altogether. The popping sounds from his lungs had grown louder and he was assailed by more frequent bouts of coughing. I searched around us for a shelter of some kind, but the best I could find was the bottom of a large tree surrounded by bushes. The thick bushes provided a protection from the breeze, and also from predators of the animal or human kind.

As gently as I could, I laid Jem down on the grassy area at the base of the tree, leaning against its trunk. His head lolled forward as if he had lost all control of it. "Jem, Jem," I yelled in a panic, holding his chin up. "Are you okay?"

Movement of his swollen eyelids told me he was still conscious. "Just tired." His voice came out raspy.

I let out the breath I'd been holding and drew him into a hug. "Hell, Jem! Never a dull moment with you," I whispered in his ear.

I heard him giggle softly. "That's me. Mr. Entertainment."

I settled myself next to him against the tree. We were pretty sheltered from sight, but it was getting cold. As with most typical spring weather, the warm day had given way to much colder temperatures at night. I pulled Jem to me so our bodies were touching. We were going to need all the heat we could get, and our flimsy indoor clothes were not going to help us.

"Are you getting frisky with me?" His words came out with difficulty.

I laughed. "Yes, because you look so sexy with all those bruises. Now shut up and sleep. You'll need your strength for tomorrow."

Jem's head dropped lower until it was resting on my breast, but instead of chiding him, I brought my hand up to his cheek and held it closer. I wanted to give him my warmth, to offer him a little extra life force through the beating of my heart. *Be well, Jem. Please, hold on.*

When my eyes fluttered open, the sun peeked shyly through the leaves of the trees. In spite of the cold and the lack of any comfort, I had slept all night. I looked down at Jem, still leaning on my chest, and my heart jumped to my throat. He was so pale it was like all the blood had drained from his face. As if he were dead.

My hand went straight to his neck to search for a pulse. "Jem, wake up," I yelled, forgetting that we wanted to remain undetectable. "Shit, Jeremy Peter, wake the fuck up!"

I felt a small movement underneath my hand. "I must look as bad as I feel." He covered my hand with his. He was very cold. "For you to curse like that. Am I dead?"

A great sob escaped my lips and I pulled him into a hug. He whimpered in my arms. "Sorry," I whispered in between sobs. "Didn't mean to hurt you. I thought you were…." I couldn't even say it out loud. Oh God! I loved this man. I loved him so much it hurt. Literally. My chest felt as if someone were sitting on it.

"Not that I want to," he said, coughing. "But shouldn't we be going?"

Against all odds, we managed to make our way through the woods undisturbed and alive. By the middle of the day we reached a main road. I sat Jem down on a big rock and walked to the edge of the road to try and catch the attention of a passing car.

No one stopped. Not that I blamed them. I doubted I would

stop for a stranger waving madly from the side of the road. I had almost given up when a police car came around the bend and stopped on the shoulder just a few yards from where we were. I ran to it.

The police officer came to help me bring Jem to the cruiser and before I knew it, he was driving us to the nearest hospital. On my way there, I relayed to him what had happened and asked him to call Detective Jarvas, who would be more qualified to explain the whole insidious affair.

"Glad to hear you're alive, girl," the detective said when he heard my voice on the line. "You gave us all a scare. How's your young man?"

"He's in bad shape," I told him. "He was beaten pretty badly." My voice caught as reality sank in. Jem was slumped over the backseat, hardly conscious. "I'm very scared for him."

"I'll meet you at the hospital," Jarvas said. "I'll call your sister and let her know you're okay. She's been driving us all crazy."

That got a giggle out of me. I could only imagine. "We'll see you at the hospital."

Jem was immediately admitted and taken away from me on a stretcher with doctors and nurses hovering over him in droves. I watched him be wheeled away with a heavy heart. I started following, but a nurse held me back. "They need to check him," she said. "And you need to be checked as well. You're bleeding."

Blood did indeed run down my arm. I couldn't even remember hurting myself. A scratch from a tree or a bush, most likely. It was nothing compared to the bleeding in my heart. Nothing at all.

In a small room in the ER, I was finally left alone after being fussed over by a legion of doctors. There was really nothing wrong with me other than a few scratches, bruises, and exhaustion. I had been practically carrying Jem for the past almost twenty-four hours. Apparently I was stronger than I had ever believed I was.

My eyes had closed and I might have been dozing, when I heard my sister's familiar voice. "Where is my crazy sister?"

I opened my eyes just in time to see her push her way through the nurses trying to block her from coming in the room. "She's resting."

"She can rest after I tell her just what I think of her," my sister said, her voice high and angry. She walked all the way to the bed and, after a quick look, threw her arms around me in a bear hug. "You scared the crap out of me."

Her arms were cutting my air. "I can't breathe, Celia," I whimpered.

Her arms loosened. "Sorry. I was just so worried," she said. "Mom and Dad are on their way from Florida."

I sighed and tilted my head. "No, why did you tell them? I didn't want them to worry."

"What if you died? How was I supposed to explain that to them? 'Sorry, Mom and Dad, we just didn't want to worry you.' It wouldn't go down well."

She sat on the edge of the bed, and we talked quietly for a few moments. "You should have listened to Marcy. She was right."

Scary as it was, she had been right. Coincidence? Or was the little witch actually capable of predicting things? "It happened right after she called." The image of the fallen officers popped in my mind. "The cops… are they dead? They were really nice men…."

Celia placed a hand on my shoulder. "They're okay. Or they will be," she said. "They're recovering from their injuries, but they're expected to make a full recovery."

"Thank goodness." I sighed. "This has been crazy."

Celia's eyes softened, and her voice went down to a whisper. "How's Jem?"

For the hundredth time this week I burst into tears. Celia gave me a hug. "I don't know," I said. "They haven't told me yet. He was beaten to a pulp, Celia…. I'm so scared I'm going to lose him."

"I'm sure he'll be fine," Celia cooed. "He's freaking strong. And stubborn. He'll be all right. I just know it."

A young nurse popped her head in the doorway. "Miss Lambert, you have a visitor."

Much to my surprise, Dave walked in, all six feet six of him, a big bouquet of flowers in his hands and the usual gorgeous smile on his lips. "Hi, sweetheart. May I come in?"

Since when was he so formal around me? "Of course. Come in."

His hug and his kiss were awkward, but sweet. "I'm so glad you're okay," he said. "I should have been there to protect you. I feel so stupid."

"Dave, you were working." I held his hand in mine. "There was no way to know what was going to happen."

"Still… I feel guilty." I noticed my sister's silence. Was she still rooting for Jem? She used to like Dave a lot. Why wasn't she saying anything?

Then, as Dave leaned over to kiss me gently on the lips, it hit me—the realization that in all this time, through everything that had happened, I hadn't given Dave a single thought. Not even once!

***

No matter how many times I told myself Jem was going to be fine, the worry had settled itself in the bottom of my stomach like a rock. All the antacids in the world weren't going to help me. The doctor had told me he was suffering from Acute Respiratory Distress Syndrome. I had immediately googled ARDS to find out more information. I was not happy with what I found.

I walked down the hallway of the hospital, dragging my IV up to the ICU where Jem was being kept for treatment and observation. I hadn't seen him since we brought him to the hospital, almost two days ago. When questioned, the doctors and nurses had thrown all kinds of words and acronyms at me—arterial blood gas tests, X-rays, bronchoscopy, CTs…. All it meant was Jem was very, very sick.

I gave my IV stand an impatient push. They had me on fluids and antibiotics because apparently I had been dehydrated when I first arrived in the ER and my blood cultures had come back positive for bacteria. As many times as I told them I was okay and I could drink my fluids instead of having them injected into my veins, no one was listening. Not even Celia, who had camped at the hospital, only taking breaks to go change clothes at home.

"But home is still almost fifty miles from here, Celia," I had told her. "What about your job?"

"They've given me some time off to be here with you," she had said. "And what's fifty miles when your sister and her best buddy need you?"

Dave's visits were pretty frequent as well. For the past two days, he had faithfully showed up for each of the two assigned visiting times in the ward. It didn't help. I was glad to see him, but it also made me feel guilty that my thoughts and my heart had been exclusively preoccupied with Jem and not him.

Jem's still extremely bruised and swollen face was visible from outside his glass-enclosed room. He had been put on a ventilator system, and tubes seemed to come out from every part of his body to connect him with all kinds of machines. The swelling had marginally subsided, and I could now see his beautiful blue eyes. I stood at the door, almost afraid to go in.

"Are you coming in, or are you just going to hold that doorway for the rest of the day?" he said, his voice throaty and hoarse.

I walked in, a forced smile plastered across my face. "You're looking better," I said, coming to settle myself on the edge of his bed. "I can see your eyes."

He giggled. "Yeah, I can actually see now," he joked. "Is that your new fashion accessory?" he asked, pointing at the IV.

"It's all the rage amongst young people now." I studied his face. He had tubes stuck to his nose and his veins, wires connecting his chest and his fingers to monitors, bandages covering most of his stomach and his head. "You should try it. It would go well with that mummy look you're going for."

He raised his hand and I held it, my fingers wrapping hungrily around his. "Are you really doing okay?" he asked, his gaze holding mine.

I nodded, not wanting to talk for fear of crying again. It was becoming a very bad habit. "I was so worried about you." *And I still am, you fool.*

With a little squeeze of my hand, he let me know he was too even if he wouldn't admit it out loud. "The doctors say I'll be fine. Just got to kick this ARDS, whatever that is. Leave it to docs to make everything sound so complicated. What's the IV for?"

We talked for a little while, me trying to get him up to speed on what had transpired, and him trying to convince me that this condition of his was nothing to be concerned about. Detective Jarvas had told me this morning that he was now convinced there was a mole in the department. Otherwise, how had they been able to figure out where we were hiding? He was putting together a plan to protect us from further problems until they caught the culprit—which, according to him, should be happening any day—but in the meantime, he had posted guards around the hospital just to be safe.

"Celia can't wait to see you," I told him. "She's been driving the whole hospital staff crazy with questions about your health."

Jem laughed, causing him to cough. "I can't wait to see her, too. I'm so glad you have her to help you through all of this." What he left unsaid was he was also happy I'd had my sister to help me through the five years without him. I felt a little pinch of the old anger in my heart.

"Dave was here also," I added, just as a barb. "He should be here soon, actually. I'm sure he's going to want to see you." Not!

His fingers tightened around mine and he brought my hand to his lips. "I'm so sorry, Emily Rose." I wasn't sure if he was asking for forgiveness for disappearing from my life or for involuntarily involving me in this mess.

"So this is where you hide to avoid your sister." Celia was standing at the doorway, a bouquet of flowers in her hand and a giant Mylar balloon in the shape of a syringe with the words "Get Well" written on it. "I've looked for you everywhere."

Jem's face brightened. "Hey, Celia, so good to see you," he said, a smile on his lips.

My sister walked in, set the bouquet on a table, and came to kiss Jem gently on the forehead, possibly the only unbruised spot on his face. "I can't tell you how good it is to see you alive and talking." She plopped herself down on the chair on the other side of the bed. "You look absolutely awful. What did you do? Have a fight with a truck and the truck won?"

"Not too far from the truth," he said, chuckling. "Those guys were built like trucks, that's for sure. I still can't believe we actually escaped. What the hell was in that bottle, Em?"

"Beats me," I replied, my hand going automatically to where the bottle used to hang. "Marcy came through though.

Bravo to the witch."

"You may want to tell her that when she comes to see you guys," Celia said. "She's been down on herself because she wasn't able to warn you of the danger sooner."

A spark of guilt lit up in my chest. "Well, chances are I would've never believed her. Even after what happened I'm still having trouble believing it all."

"I told you she was the real thing," Celia protested.

A noise from the doorway made us all look up. Dave was standing there with a teddy bear crushed against his chest and looking just a little forlorn. "Hi, guys," he said, finally. "Hope you don't mind me crashing the party."

Instinctively I dropped Jem's hand. "Of course we don't mind. Come in." I sounded just a little too chirpy. My guilty conscience was giving me a hard time.

Dave took a couple long steps and kissed me on the lips, long and hard. I didn't dare look at Jem for fear of what I may read in his expression. When our lips separated, my face was burning and I felt a sudden need to dig a huge hole to hide in. *Get it together, woman. This is your boyfriend, after all.* But the beaten-up man witnessing this hot kiss was Jem. It just didn't feel right.

Turning to Jem, Dave smiled and offered his hand for a shake. Jem, hesitantly at first, lifted his hand to him. "How are you doing, Jeremy?" Dave said, shaking the IV-connected hand a bit too enthusiastically. "I want to thank you for being there for my girl when I wasn't."

The irony of those words did not escape Jem, whose lips curved into a little smile. "That was my pleasure," he replied with a sly glance in my direction. I fought the urge to stick my tongue out at him again. "Nice of you to come and see us."

"How could I not?" Dave said, his hand cradling the back of my head in a caress. "This is my favorite girl, and I wasn't there when she needed me. Can't tell you how guilty I feel."

"All right, all right," Celia exclaimed, waving her hands. "Enough of this guilt fest. No one is to blame for this mess other than the freaking criminals who did all this. So stop this I-feel-so-guilty crap and let's have some fun."

We all stared at her, surprised and confused. "Fun? We're at the hospital. What are you talking about?" I asked the question burning on everybody's tongue.

From her gigantic bag, Celia produced a deck of cards. "There are four of us. Poker, anyone?" she said with a grin.

Jem lifted his arm up in the air, rattling all the wires and tubes attached to him. "I say we play strip poker," he said. "Not that I have many clothing items to remove but again, I don't intend to lose."

Dave looked at him and then at me, as if wondering whether Jem was serious or joking. I laughed. "He couldn't be more serious," I said. "I think they're giving him some strong meds."

We played poker—the regular kind—until a nurse came to shoo us out of the room. It was time for some more tests and for Jem to rest. In spite of his strong protests, we all left the room and went to sit in a visiting area nearby. Dave had looped his arm around my waist and held me protectively against him all the time. My guilt only grew with each caress, each word of concern. Oh my God, what had I gotten myself into?

Celia had gone off to bug the doctors about my care—or so she claimed. I suspected she had a crush on one of the young residents on my ward. I was left alone with Dave, my heart beating fast from the anxiety. It caused me to feel I was lying to him. Even though I really wasn't. I did love Dave. Very much. But not like I loved Jem. I didn't think I would ever be able to love anyone ever again the way I loved my best friend.

"When I think of what could have happened to you, I feel so angry," Dave said, his hands holding mine. "I just don't know what I would do if I lost you."

Not helping the guilt trip, Dave. Not helping at all.

"Nothing happened." Other than Jem being beaten within an inch of his life. "I'm fine and I should be going home very soon. I miss my class and my own bed."

He pulled me toward him in a tight embrace. "Maybe I should move in with you." That floored me! Where did that come from? In all the time we'd been dating, that subject had never really come up. Why now? "That way I could be close if you needed me."

Shaking, I hid my face in his shoulder. I did not want him to see my expression. "That's very sweet of you, Dave, but we have our professional lives and I really don't need someone watching over me."

I must have sounded a bit too rough because he pulled me back and looked me in the eye. "Are you saying moving in together is out of the question?" *No, no, no… why now?*

"I'm just not ready to talk about it right now," I fudged. "So much has happened in these past few days, my head is reeling from it all. I need time to relax and clear my mind.

Surely you can understand that, right?"

He nodded, his honest, handsome face very close to mine. "Of course, sweetheart. I'm sorry." *Don't apologize. Please, don't apologize.* "I don't know what I was thinking. You need your space and time. We'll talk about this later."

Or never.

Before I could move away, he came in for a kiss. I had always loved the feeling of his generous lips on mine, but now they felt flat. I did not want to lock lips with him. Not now. Maybe never again. What was wrong with me? This was the same sweet man I had been dating and making love to for the past two years, and now, out of the blue, it felt awkward to be the center of his affection.

Thankfully, Dave had to leave shortly after that. His business couldn't run itself, and it was still quite a long ride from the hospital to town. We said our farewells back in my room just in time for my sister to come back. Celia was flushed and I could have sworn her lipstick was slightly smudged. What had she been up to?

"So, what do you want to do now?" she asked, rubbing her hands together as if plotting the caper of the century.

"I would very much like for you to introduce me to the doctor who has been exchanging kisses with you while your sister is languishing in her hospital bed."

She threw a pillow at me. So, I was right after all.

Chapter Ten

Angels in Hospital Gowns

Her leopard-print palazzo pants kept distracting me. Sometimes it was very hard to keep your focus in the presence of Marcy, the witch. Her clothing was as hypnotizing as a magician's watch. Today she had topped her outfit with a pretty, plain white shirt, tied into a knot by her waist, and her crazy, red, frizzy hair was marginally controlled by a crocheted black beanie. Where did this girl shop for clothes?

"You are not listening to me," she said in an accusatory tone.

"Sorry, Marcy." I refocused my attention. "Are you saying you think we're safe now?"

"Your auras are clean," she said with a very serious face.

"Did you wash them?" Celia threw me a look that could only be described as metal-melting. "Bad joke. I just have trouble… believing in that stuff."

The little witch adjusted the waist of her pants. "I know,

and that's okay as long as you listen to me the next time I tell you to run."

I couldn't argue with that. Coincidence or not, it was just slightly spooky that she had warned me of danger minutes before it had actually happened.

"I promise to give your warnings the utmost consideration," I said by way of a compromise, pushing the IV tube out of the way. "Can you see in your crystal ball when they'll remove this contraption from my arm?"

Marcy laughed. I loved the way she laughed. It was genuine and heartfelt. "Silly. Witches don't use crystal balls." Then again, she seemed to have a hard time identifying sarcasm when she heard it.

"Mom and Dad called," Celia said, fussing over me. "They're back safe and sound. They wanted me to tell you that they still have that god-awful flamingo you gave them when they first moved to Florida. They say it turned out to be super helpful scaring the gators away."

I giggled. It *was* a seriously hideous yard flamingo. My parents had left the day before, after a short visit. They wanted to stay longer, but I fought them all the way. No point in them worrying themselves sick when I was perfectly fine. Maybe a little shaken, kind of like James Bond's drinks, but not stir-crazy.

Jem's parents had arrived in town with mine. Leave it to parents to plot a mass attack on their children. Smooth talker that he was, Jem had been able to convince his parents to go back to their laid-back retiree life along with mine after a very short visit. Both sets of parents had moaned and groaned, but in the end they gave in. Now with them back in sunny Florida, we both could breathe a little easier.

"It's time for my visit with Jem, so if you ladies would kindly remove yourselves from my room, I would deeply appreciate it." I pushed the sheets aside.

Celia gave me a pointed look. "I thought you wanted to stay away from him," she said.

"We were kidnapped together. Twice!" I swung my legs off the bed. "It's a little late for that."

My sister rushed to help me get out of the bed. "I'm just worried that you're getting too close to Jem and losing perspective."

I readjusted the IV bag on the stand. "I thought you liked Jem." I was confused by her attitude.

"I love Jem and I would love nothing better than you guys getting together," she said, straightening my hospital gown. "But I also know how you are and how you would never leave Dave, no matter how much you love Jem."

"I love Dave," I protested weakly.

"Yes, you do." Celia was staring at me with that I-know-you-better-than-you-know-yourself look. "And you would be miserable for the rest of your life because you wouldn't have the heart to tell him you're in love with someone else."

I prickled. "Jem and I are just friends—"

Celia crossed her arms across her chest. "Are you telling me you guys spent all that time together—alone—and nothing happened?" Uh-oh, she had that truth serum stare.

I shook my head in denial. "Nothing happened." Then I glanced at her. "Almost nothing."

My evil sister pointed her finger at me. "Ah-ha! I knew it! You guys did the nasty."

My face contorted in horror. "No, oh my God, Celia, no!" I yelled. "We absolutely did not do any such thing." Okay, we may have come close, but no cigar. "We kissed, that's all."

"That's all?" Marcy exclaimed in unison with my sister. "A kiss is the deepest manifestation of love."

Giving up, I threw my hands in the air and left the room huffing and puffing. Well-intentioned women with the most annoying habit of sticking their noses where they did not belong. Let them entertain themselves while I visited my beaten-up friend… whom I deeply, truly, hopelessly loved. Hell! What was I going to do?

The nurse was just finishing up changing his bandages, and as I walked in I spied the ugly bruises staining his muscular chest with a purplish black. "Nice colors there, my friend," I quipped while my heart was plummeting to my feet.

Jem looked up. The swelling around his eyes had subsided substantially, and I could now clearly see his beautiful blue eyes—still bloodshot but open at least. "So, we're back to being friends?" At my quizzical look, he added, "From frenemies and occasional bed buddies."

The nurse threw me a quick glance and smiled, amused. I felt the need to explain. "It's not what you think. He just means we had to share a bed because it was the only one available." The nurse smiled wider. "Nothing happened. Really."

I don't think the lovely lady in white was buying it. How could she? I was having trouble myself. Not when my heart was telling me something very different.

"No funny business." She waved her long finger at me. "He must get as much rest as he can." She left with another smile dancing in her eyes.

"See what you did?" I said, approaching the bed. "Now she thinks we're an item."

"Why does that bother you so much?" Jem had been taken off the ventilator, but he was still connected to all kinds of monitoring machines. The doctors seemed to think he was out of the woods, so to speak. But they preferred to err on the side of caution.

"Because it's not true." I avoided his piercing eyes. "If Dave hears these… notions, he'll get upset. I don't want to hurt him."

Suddenly, his smile vanished and a somber expression came over his face. "Won't you hurt him more if you make him believe he's the one you truly love when he's not?"

"And what makes you think that's what's happening?" I grumbled, irritation growing like a roaring fire inside of me. "Why does everybody think they know what's going on inside my heart better than me?"

Silence fell around us as I stood by the side of his bed, panting as if I had just run a marathon. The ever-present tears of late were burning in my eyes again. My conflicted self fought with the choice of either running out of the room or finding the comfort I craved in Jem's arms.

In a quick move, Jem took hold of my hand and pulled me closer. "I held you against my heart and you've held me against yours. You may have not spoken the words, but your heart did. My heart did, too. You can't deny it."

I pulled my hand away from his. "Jeremy Peter, you are full of shit and you know it!" I said, my voice a low growl. "No matter what you say, if you really loved me you wouldn't have run after Tina all the way to another continent." I hoped he wouldn't notice I wasn't denying what he had said about my heart's desires.

"I didn't run after her!" he said emphatically. "I ran in the same direction. There's a difference."

My heart galloped like a wild horse, leaving me gasping for air. "Are you going to lie there and tell me you never slept with Tina? That all these years, your relationship was purely platonic?" Did I really want him to tell me what I already knew? It was almost as if I needed him to hurt me, so I could justify denying myself his love.

His hesitation spoke volumes and felt like the stabbing of a thousand knives straight to the chest. "I can't," he said in a small voice, his eyes falling from mine. "You know very well that I can't."

Bleeding inside and with tears blurring my vision, I took a deep breath and spat out the words. "Right! Exactly! You don't know what love is."

I'm not sure how I managed to run all the way to my room with the IV stand trailing behind me, but I did. Thankfully neither Celia nor Marcy was there. I threw myself on the bed, my face buried in the pillow, and cried. Five years of wondering what had happened, and even more of loving him in secret while he dated every skirt in town, burned in my chest. The last few weeks of yearning for something that came too little, too late poured out into the pillow in a torrent of liquid pain.

I felt arms encircle me and knew that my sister was back. I would recognize those arms anywhere. Through the years we had comforted each other more often than we would like to admit. "Shhh," she cooed in my ear. "Everything will be all right."

I held on to her as if to a lifeline and cried my heart out some more. "I hate him. I hate him so much." I did. I hated him for leaving me. I hated him for stealing my heart. I hated him for coming back. And for each *I hate him* I had an *I love him,* because one didn't seem to go without the other. Not for Jem, my best friend who had been there for me so many times in the past I had lost count. The boy, and then the man, I had fallen in love with was not the villain I wanted to believe he was—he was just human, flawed like everyone else. No more, no less.

The smell of something sweet and warm reached my nostrils. "Drink this, girl." Marcy was standing by us, a cup of something hot and steamy in her hands. "This will soothe your heart and your soul."

I doubted that anything could do that, but at that point I was willing to try just about anything that had the slightest chance of pulling me out of the misery pit I had dug myself into. I wiped the tears that still lingered in my eyes and took the cup from her.

"Jem called me," my sister said suddenly. "He said you were hurting and that, since he couldn't get out of bed and do it himself, I should come and give you a hug."

I'm sure I looked utterly pitiful, with blotchy eyes and a

snotty nose. I sniffed and took a long sip of the tea. It was very fragrant and bitter with a faint taste of strawberries. In spite of my doubts, I started feeling better immediately. This witch had some skills after all.

"I know you don't want to hear it, and it's really not my place to say this." Marcy pushed her sliding glasses up the bridge of her nose. "But if you guys love each other—and it's obvious that you do—why not just give in? You're fighting your own heart and that's not a good place to be."

My sister answered for me. "The problem, Marcy, is Dave. She doesn't want to break his heart."

Marcy wrinkled her tiny nose and squinted. "But Celia," she said, lowering her voice, "haven't you told her about…?" She was interrupted by my sister's distinctive look of death. What was going on?

"What Marcy means is that maybe you should just talk to Dave about it." Nice save. She was definitely hiding something.

I must have been under some kind of spell because even though my brain was telling me I should inquire further, I let it go. So very unlike me.

"Dave asked me if he could move in with me." I took another sip from the miraculous tea.

Celia's eyes opened so wide, I thought her eyeballs would pop out. "What?" She was practically screaming. "He did what?"

I took another tiny sip from the delicious, tart concoction and sighed. "He wanted to move in so he could take care of me."

Marcy made a move as if to say something, but she was brusquely interrupted by my sister. "When did this happen?"

What was in this tea? I felt as if I were walking on clouds. A giggle escaped my lips. "A couple days ago," I said with what had to be a very silly grin. "What in heaven's name is in this tea? I feel high as a kite."

The red-haired witch laughed. "Yes, it is very relaxing and potent," she said. "I gave you an extra-strong dose. Glad to see it's working."

Celia looked at Marcy and frowned. "Are you sure she's okay? She's acting as if she's drunk."

With an enthusiastic nod, Marcy took the empty cup out of my hands. "She's fine. In fact, now might be the best time to tell her about Dave."

That made my ears perk up a bit. "What about Dave? Is he here? He's such a sweet man," I babbled on. I could actually hear myself saying these things as if I were watching myself from a distance. "He doesn't deserve this. I'm a bad person." I burst out laughing. "Marcy, did anybody ever tell you that you wear the weirdest clothes?"

Marcy laughed again. In the back of my mind—way back—I knew I wasn't making any sense, but I couldn't stop it. I felt so relaxed and happy.

Whispering reached my ears, but I couldn't hear the words. My sister was busy telling the little witch something. She looked worried or mad, not sure which. Nothing was making much sense to me at that moment.

"Hey, witch!" I called, falling backward into my pillow. "What's in this tea?"

"Skullcap and strawberries," Marcy replied, winking at Celia.

"Well, the caps of those skulls are something, let me tell you," I rambled on. "You should bottle it and sell it."

I turned on my side and curled into a fetal position. "Feeling very sleepy…," I said.

Right before falling asleep, I thought I heard my sister say, "I can't tell her now. She's too fragile." But I was probably dreaming already.

Sometime during the night, around the time when hospital hallways become this dreamlike world, I got out of bed and walked to Jem's room in the ICU. The undercover policemen who had been watching his room like hawks didn't bother to stop me. By now they knew exactly who I was.

Jem was fast asleep and I watched him silently for a long time. His golden curls were spread on the white pillow now that they had removed his head bandages. His face, so savagely abused, was relaxed and almost back to its normal shape and size. I used to spend a lot of time watching him sleep when we were younger, fascinated as I was with his ability to sleep soundly and peacefully through just about anything. These many years later, I was still in awe of the way he slept with total abandon, even here in the hospital and after having gone through such a traumatic experience.

In spite of my earlier anger, I smiled. This was my Jem, my together-forever pal of childhood and teen years.

Quietly, I climbed in bed with him, careful of all the wires and tubes, pulling the thin blankets over both of us. I settled myself against his side, my head on his shoulder, hand across his chest. I closed my eyes and listened. His heart sang against my ear, a life-giving beat that both energized and lulled me to sleep. Unconsciously, his arm came to rest on top of mine, like it had done so many times in the past. It felt so right.

Tomorrow I would face reality, but for now I was in heaven in the arms of an angel. All was well.

Chapter Eleven

Betrayal and Revenge

The police decided to keep me in the hospital the full week and a half even though I had been cleared for release less than a week after I was admitted. It was easier to keep us both safe if we were in the same place, they told me. Now that Jem had finally been declared healed enough to go home, I was also free to go. Or at least, I was free to leave the hospital. They were still going to keep us together and under twenty-four-hour surveillance until either Tina was brought back from France, or wherever she was, to give her testimony in court or the one to blame for this mess was behind bars. Jem was in danger until then, and so was I by association. Because of the possible mole in the department, Detective Jarvas had decided there was not much point in taking us to a safe house and was going to allow us to stay at my place, as long as we complied with their rules and didn't stray without some kind of escort.

"Visitors will be restricted to a very small list of friends and family," the detective had told us earlier that day. "I understand that Ms. Stregabrutta—Tina—has decided to come out of hiding to testify and will be arriving soon. After that your lives will return to normal." What a joke! Normal! As if. Nothing would ever be normal again.

As part of the "deal"—as if we really had much say in the matter—I had been given permission to drive to Allentown where Dave had been working on this mysterious and all-consuming new landscaping job. I wanted to surprise him. I felt so guilty for all the feelings in my heart and my traitorous thoughts that I had to do something nice for him. He had taken my hesitation about moving in together pretty hard, it seemed. The last few times he had visited, he'd seemed distant and much colder than normal. I wanted to make it right again somehow.

"I will surprise him on location," I had told my sister the day before.

Surprisingly, she frowned. "Do you think that's a good idea?"

"Of course I do." I looked at her suspiciously. She had been acting very strangely lately—even for her. "Why else would I do it if I didn't think it was a good idea?"

Even stranger, Marcy visited me later that day to bring me another one of her potions. "Wear this at all times," she instructed, holding up a little glass vial in her hand. "It will protect you from bad vibes. And it wouldn't hurt if you carried some skullcap tincture with you for emergencies."

What emergencies was she talking about? It wasn't like I was walking around panicking over everything that happened.

I had been kidnapped twice in the past month and I never once freaked out—not completely anyway. Celia and the little witch were up to something, but I was too preoccupied with my own love life to think about it too much.

Jem was packed into the ambulance in a wheelchair in spite of his loud protests. "You need to rest longer. Your ankle is still not 100 percent healed, and your lungs are in serious need of a vacation," I told him, after a lengthy conversation with one of his doctors.

I climbed up front with the EMT who was driving. The poor man was not happy. Apparently he had been grilled like a criminal by the security detail in charge of our safety. He wasn't the only one though. Everybody in the hospital who had any contact with us, from doctors to janitors, had suffered through long interviews and intrusive background checks. Another thing to make me feel guilty.

My house would be our hidey-hole for the near future. I was not completely sure how that had come about, but one minute we had been discussing possible locations, and the next my place had been "volunteered" for it. I didn't mind too much. At least I would be home, surrounded by the comfort of my own things. It was the company that unnerved me. Having Jem as a roommate again was not a great idea by any stretch of the imagination.

"You'll be in separate rooms," Miss Obvious had said. Celia seemed to be almost giddy about the situation. "There's nothing wrong with being under the same roof."

No, of course not. Unless you incessantly crave your roommate's body and soul. Let's face it. Putting Jem in an enclosed space with me was like locking a starved vampire in with a breathing human; it wouldn't end well.

Marcy and my sister were at my place when we got there. They had been "tidying up," which in their alien language meant they had been smudging the house with sage and hiding protective amulets. I could almost guarantee I would find a love talisman somewhere in there. They had prepared the spare bedroom for Jem and furnished it with a television set brought from God knew where.

The two of them fussed over poor Jem, who seemed utterly overwhelmed with the attention. I was almost sorry for him. He had not been around my sister for a long time. He had forgotten what a pain she could be. I grabbed a cup of coffee from the kitchen and decided to take pity on him. While I leaned against the doorway, Jem threw me a look that screamed *help*. I laughed and came to his rescue.

"All right, ladies." I pushed my way through the two crazy women in the room. "Jem needs his rest. Doctor's orders. Shoo." Reluctantly, they obeyed me and left to roost in the living room instead. I looked at my bewildered friend with a grin. "I thought you enjoyed the ladies' attention."

He shook his head and stretched his leg on top of a small stool the dynamic duo had padded with a giant cushion. "They are something, aren't they?"

I offered him the coffee as a peace offering. "They're something, all right," I agreed. "I just don't know what exactly."

"It's nice to be out of that hospital though, isn't it?" he asked, taking the mug to his lips.

I nodded and sat beside him on the love seat. "We never talked about what happened, Jem," I said, lowering my voice so the two crazy hens in the living room wouldn't hear me. "We should, you know? You went through hell out there."

Jem lowered his eyes. "I'm fine," he said, brushing off the subject. "It's over."

"No, it's not over." The faded, but still very obvious, bruises on his face were a constant reminder of what had happened. "I know that inside you're still hurting. I am."

He put down the coffee mug and held my hands. "I'm sorry. Of course you must have felt terrified. I've been too preoccupied to notice...."

Pulling a little on his hands, I made him look at me. "I'm not talking about me. I'm hurting because I saw what they did to you. I have spent many a night awake thinking of how you must have felt when they beat you up. They could have killed you."

My voice must have reflected the pain I felt inside, because his eyes softened and watered. "But they didn't, did they?" he said. "I'm here. I'm alive and I'm not going to dwell on what happened. It's in the past. I want to think of the future instead." He smiled. "You know what they say—what doesn't kill you...."

"Makes you stronger," I finished. "If you ever need to talk, I'm here."

I joined my sister and friend while Jem stretched out for a nap. I was itching to leave to go see Dave. I had this notion that if I saw him outside the hospital, things would go back to normal—that I would once again feel the warmth I used to feel when I was with him. Detective Jarvas had made me promise I would wait until he himself came to escort me to Dave's work site. He was taking his sweet time.

"I really think you should just call Dave and tell him you're home," Celia said, not for the first time. "It's dangerous for you to be driving around."

"You are full of it." I put down the book I was reading. "For some reason, you don't want me to go see him. What is it?"

It was impossible not to notice the furtive look between her and Marcy. "I really think it's too risky, sis. Just stay put and he'll come and see you."

Marcy looked at me and then at my sister, biting her lip so hard it turned purple. "You should tell her, Celia," the young witch said.

"Tell me what?" I yelled, frustrated. "What the hell is going on?"

A loud honk prevented my sister from answering. Visibly relieved by the interruption, she jumped out of her seat and ran to the window. "It's Detective Jarvas."

With a sour taste in my mouth, I grabbed my jacket from the coat hanger and opened the door. "You will tell me when I come back," I threatened before closing the door behind me.

The drive to Allentown was almost an hour, and traffic was heavy. It was going to be a long drive.

"How is our young man doing?" the detective asked, his eyes glued to the road ahead.

"Stubborn and reluctant to talk about what happened," I answered. "Is it normal for a victim of a violent crime to refuse to talk about it?"

His hands kept going to the pack of cigarettes in his shirt pocket, as if to make sure they were still there. "Very normal. By not talking about it, he's avoiding reliving the trauma," he explained. "Give him time. He'll eventually open up."

"You can smoke if you like," I told him, realizing he wasn't doing it for my benefit. "Just crack the window open."

"Thank you." With a grateful smile, he opened the window and pulled a cigarette from the pack. "Jeremy is a brave young man." Smoke began spiraling up and out the window.

"Yes, he is," I said, twisting my hands on my lap. "But annoying as hell, too."

The detective drove like a madman, and our trip was a lot shorter than I had expected. The address I had been given as Dave's work site turned out to be a row of high-end condos downtown. Surprised, I got out of the car and, closely followed by the policeman, I walked into the building.

"Weird," I mumbled to no one in particular. "This doesn't look like Dave's usual venue."

The elevator took us to the top floor, where Dave's secretary had told me he would be. When the doors opened, I understood why he was working there. The whole rooftop had been turned into a landscaped paradise with a lawn, pebbled paths, and even a small greenhouse. I was just admiring the beauty of the work in progress when a movement in a corner to the right of us caught my eye.

My legs gave away underneath me as my brain struggled to reconcile what I was seeing with everything I had always believed about my boyfriend. Dave was entwined in a very intimate embrace with a blonde woman I had never seen before. They were both in some level of undress, and so involved in their lovemaking that neither of them noticed they were being watched.

"Dave!" His name escaped my lips as a scream of anguish. My chest hurt as if I had just been stabbed. I couldn't breathe. Detective Jarvas rushed to support me as I fell to the floor and faded into oblivion.

"Are you okay?" the detective was asking me as I came to sometime later. I opened my eyes slowly, woozy and dizzy, as if the whole building were moving under me. The sunlight burnt my eyes and I raised a hand to cover them. "I knew it was too soon to get you out of the house. You need a few more days' rest."

Shaking my head made me even dizzier. "I'm all right," I said. "I have very low blood pressure and I tend to pass out often." It wasn't totally true. I did have low blood pressure, but it took a pretty good shock to make me pass out like that. "Where is he?"

Jarvas looked confused. "Who?"

"My boyfriend," I answered, the words bitter in my mouth. "The one making out with that woman."

His mouth fell open and he hesitated for a second. "That was *your* boyfriend?" I nodded. "The son of a bitch! He went to get you a glass of water. I'm going to kick his ass."

Unsuccessfully, I tried to stand up. "Get me out of here, Detective Jarvas. Please," I begged. "I don't want to see him. Not now."

The policeman slid his arm under mine and gently pulled

me up to my feet. "You probably should rest a while," he said.

I shook my head again, another wave of nausea overwhelming my senses. "No, please take me out of here. I can't handle seeing him right now." I must have sounded really desperate because the good cop practically carried me to the elevator and out to the car.

As we drove away I saw the tall figure of my traitorous boyfriend standing by the front door of the building. I gagged, and the car sped down the street away from there.

During our drive back home, the detective respected my need for silence, only talking once every so often to find out whether I was still breathing. Betrayal seared into my heart like acid. I had always trusted Dave. I had always loved him and respected him. Why would he betray me like this? Was there something about me that attracted acts of deception? Jem had left me without a word after a lifetime of friendship and now Dave. Was I always going to be the one left behind? Alone and empty?

When I was dropped at home and into the arms of my sister, my eyes were still dry. The one person who had been crying over the smallest thing for the past few weeks could not shed a tear now. Numb, I was not. My whole being burned with an intensity I didn't know was possible, but the tears wouldn't come. I was not sure my heart could handle any more pain.

"I'm sorry, sis." Celia held me against her. "I didn't know how to tell you."

My head popped up. "You knew?" I almost yelled. "You knew he was cheating on me and didn't tell me?" Outrage coursed through my body, and I began shaking violently.

Another betrayal.

"I was hoping Dave would tell you himself," Celia said, her head bent. "After everything that happened, I didn't want to add more to your plate."

I rubbed my eyes. "I just walked in on my boyfriend making out with another woman," I said, anger coloring my voice. "Do you think that it was better that way? Do you know how it feels to watch the person you have trusted and shared your life with for two years stick his tongue down someone else's throat? Well, do you?"

Celia had tears in her eyes, and a part of me wanted to hug her and tell her I understood why she did it. I did understand. I knew now why she practically threw me into Jem's arms. She was hoping I would decide to break up with my two-timing lover and be happy with my childhood friend. I did understand, but I was very angry. Red-hot, blindingly angry.

"Go home, Celia." I stood up and pointed to the door. "I need to be alone. Go!"

After retrieving her purse and keys, my sister left, throwing a last glance at me. It had been a long time since I had been angry at her, and never quite like this. I would make amends later, but for now I needed to surround myself with the cocoon of rage, protected from coherent but unsettling thoughts.

"What's going on?" I heard Jem yell from his room. We must have woken him up.

I didn't want to talk to him either. "Leave me alone," I yelled back as I walked into my room and slammed the door behind me.

***

My phone had more missed calls than I could count. Once in a while I peeked at the list; most of them were from the traitor, but there were also calls from my sister, Marcy, and even my roommate. I had been stewing in my own juices for more than twenty-four hours, and I was yet to shed a tear. That small detail baffled me more than anything else. What was wrong with me? I had let my anger take over the grief, and that was not like me at all.

After a night of minimum sleep, I concocted revenge plans in my brain. I was not a vengeful person, but this whole thing had stirred such anger, such wrath in me, all I could think of was getting back at my treacherous boyfriend. Blood and murder had been part of some of the plans, but I knew those to be purely wistful. No matter how mad and how tempting it was, I would never be capable of murder. There were other ways, things I would have never thought of doing before, but that now emerged from my feverish imagination as tempting as alcohol to an addict.

"Open this door!" It was Jem. In the back of my mind I knew he must be really worried, because it was still painful for him to walk on that leg. For him to have attempted the short walk from his room to mine reeked of desperation. "He's not worthy of your pain. Come on, Emily Rose. Come out and talk to me."

Go away, Jem.

"Celia is sick with worry, and so am I," he said. Well, my

sister had betrayed me as well. So let her be worried. She deserved it. "Come out, Em, please."

Eventually he gave up and I heard him limp back to his room. Didn't they understand? With each betrayal, small or large, my heart had filled with pain just a little more, until there was no more room. I had no choice but to let it all burst out in a tidal wave of resentment and rage. I was not in control anymore. The wise, cautious, and kind woman in me had been pushed so far down in the recesses of my brain and heart that a bulldozer wouldn't be enough to dig her out.

I spent the rest of the day plotting, allowing my rage to grow to epic proportions. By the time the dark of night rolled over, my heart had turned black and my brain had quit functioning normally. I was a walking stupid-bomb. I was aware of it to a certain extent, but it was almost as if I were watching myself from afar, a passive onlooker with no will and no power to react.

The house was very quiet. Jem must have been asleep because his TV was silent. I opened the door to his room as quietly as I could manage and stepped inside. Closing the door behind me, I stood for a moment adjusting my eyes to the semidarkness. I could guess, rather than see, my friend's sleeping form on the bed, the weak light from the alarm clock blinking to the sound of my own heart.

I crawled into bed, sitting on my bent legs beside Jem, watching as his bruised chest rose with each breath he took. A new kind of anger rose within me. Anger against the men who had done that to him, who had disfigured him with their fists and their feet. I leaned forward and brushed my hand across his chest and then his face. In spite of my anger, it was a gentle caress. One that carried all the love I'd had for him for years.

I bent down further and covered his lips with mine. I could feel the rough spots that marked where his skin had broken, and a new stirring grew inside of me. My tongue parted his lips and began exploring the warmth and sweetness of his mouth. The flicker of flame in my belly exploded into a full-blown fire when he responded in kind.

Realizing he wasn't dreaming, Jem pulled away from me and looked me in the eye. "Emily Rose?" he said, his voice still slurred from sleep. "What are you doing?"

I crushed my lips against his in response. Forgetting his injuries, I pulled myself on top of him, drunk with desire. Underneath me I could feel his own desire growing with each stroke of my tongue against his.

Suddenly, he pushed me away. "Stop! Stop this." Surprised by his reaction, I could only stare. "Why are you doing this?

"What do you mean, why? Isn't this what you wanted all along?" I yelled at him, anxious to bury my anger and my frustration into lovemaking.

"You have no idea how much I want it," he said, keeping me at bay. "But not like this."

I slid my body along his and a moan escaped his lips. Oh, he so wanted this! Discarding the blanket that separated us, I went to work untying the strings in his pants. "Like what?" I asked, suggestively brushing my hand across the scarred muscles of his abdomen.

"Stop, Emily Rose! Please…." He sounded so desperate that I did stop for a moment. "If we go through with this right now, you won't be able to look me in the eye tomorrow. This moment will grow into a wall between us." Was he right? Would this destroy whatever hope there was for us? "I want us to get close, not further apart."

"I want this, Jem," I said. It wasn't a lie. I did want this. I had wanted it since we were in college, but then Jem had left, and Dave had entered my life. *Dave*! My anger came back full force. "I want to make love to you, Jem. I thought you wanted it, too."

"God, Em. Of course I do," he said, his voice a bit lower. "But this is not about me and you. You're angry. This is about you and Dave. I don't want Dave with us in bed. When we make love, I want to be the only one in your thoughts. I want you to do it because you want me, not because you want to hurt Dave."

The tears that had been absent for the past twenty-four hours made a sudden appearance, running down my cheeks like rivers of heartache. He was right, of course. This wasn't fair on him or even me. Tomorrow I would regret it all bitterly.

"It hurts, Jem," I said with a sob. "It hurts so much."

Jem sat up and held me against him. "I know, I know," he whispered in my ear. Then he pulled me down until we were lying side by side, my head buried in the crook of his neck. "I'm here for you, Emily Rose. I won't ever go away again. I promise."

I cried for a while. Jem seemed to have a knack for releasing the waterworks in me. Little by little, I calmed down. The heat of his body against mine soothed my pain. His hand, caressing my head and face, comforted my soul.

"I'm still mad at you," I said, anger gone from my voice.

He laughed softly. "You have good reason to be." He kissed the top of my head. "And once I'm a little more healed, I'm going to kick Dave's ass, and then I'm going to thank him."

I raised my head a little to look at him. "Thank him?"

A little, wicked smile curved the corner of his lips. "For being stupid enough to clear the way for me."

"I hate when you're adorable," I said, even though I loved it. It made me love him that much more. He kissed me then. Not the down-your-throat kiss I had performed on him earlier, but a gentle, warm-your-toes lip suckling that made me sparkle to the core and left me panting for more.

"Just to remind you what you could be getting frequently if you ever stop being mad at me and allow me to love you full-time," he said with infuriating logic. "Good night, Emily Rose. I need my beauty sleep."

I settled back on his shoulder but couldn't go to sleep. My body was on fire. I realized with a jolt that I hadn't thought of Dave or how angry I was at everybody in almost an hour. It seemed like Jem was more than a friend—he was also a miracle worker.

Chapter Twelve

Forgiveness and New Beginnings

"You're going to be mad." Those words never preceded anything good. I squinted at him, bracing myself for what was coming next. "I called Celia. She's coming over to talk to you."

My teeth were clenched so tightly together, my jaw started to hurt. "I don't want to talk to her."

Liar! I did want to talk to her. I missed my sister something awful. It had been almost a week since the whole Dave fiasco and, even though I was still mad at her, I was ready to forgive and forget.

"Come on, Em." Jem was walking easier now. He still favored one side, but he could at least walk around without major pain. His breathing was normal and the visiting nurse had just removed all his bandages that morning. "She's your sister."

"She knew about Dave and she didn't tell me!" My heart

still dropped every time I thought about it. I wasn't sure which betrayal hurt the most: Dave's or my sister's.

Jem took a deep breath. He looked delicious—sweatpants that hung low on his hips and a plain black T-shirt that seemed tattooed to his chest muscles. "She was trying to protect you." He combed his curls with the tips of his fingers. "Like you, she thought that Dave would be decent enough to tell you himself. But he didn't, and she left it until it was too late. You have to see that she did it with good intentions."

"You shouldn't stick your nose where it doesn't belong, mister," I said, affecting what I hoped was an angry tone of voice. "You're very annoying."

He grabbed me and pulled me to him. His face came down. "You love when I butt in," he said, his lips sending shivers down my spine as they touched the sensitive skin of my ear. His hands tightened around me and I felt, against my backside, the telltale sign we were playing with fire. "Hell, now you got me all hot and bothered."

Laughing nervously, I disentangled myself from his arms and sat on the couch, my legs too weak to carry me. "So, when is she getting here?"

As if on cue, the doorbell rang. I raised an eyebrow in question. Jem laughed. "You better open the door," he said. He looked down at his pants. "I'm in no shape to be seen. I'll be in my room, cooling off."

My cheeks burned as he walked into his room, obviously more than a little aroused. I stood on shaking legs and opened the door to my sister.

Celia looked positively crestfallen and young. I was

transported to our childhood, when she would look at me with those round blue eyes and make me do whatever it was she wanted me to do. I could never resist those puppy eyes. Without hesitation, I drew her into a hug.

"I'm sorry, Em," she said, her voice shaking. "I just didn't want to hurt you."

"Shush, it's okay," I said, rocking her side to side. "I know. I'm sorry, too. I overreacted. I was just shocked. It was all so unexpected."

We sat together on the couch, holding hands and talking in whispers like we used to do when we were little girls. It was better than therapy. My heart felt lighter, my anger dissipated—mostly—and I felt hope again.

The thing with Dave was hard, very hard, but I wasn't really in love with him. I loved him, but not in a romantic way. Not in a together-forever way. That love was, and had always been, reserved for my best friend, Jem. I was in love with the idea of Dave, the good, stable guy that could turn me into goo with a kiss. The man who would always be there, a solid figure in an ever-changing life. As it turned out, Dave was just as flawed as everybody else. The man I thought would always be loyal and present had been making out with another woman while I was a prisoner. Yes, I had also kind of made out with Jem, but I had stopped myself. I had made the very conscious decision to let go of the love of my life and choose Dave, the one I could count on—or so I thought, anyway.

"Where is Jem?" my sister suddenly asked, looking around the room as if he could be hiding behind a piece of furniture.

"He's in the bedroom." I blushed furiously. "He was

having some… anxiety issues." I cleared my throat. "Jem, Celia's here. Can you come out?"

The door opened and Jem came out, a big smile on his face. Celia jumped off the couch and ran to throw herself in his arms.

"Ouch, girly," he whimpered. "Watch out for the bruises." But his laugh belied his words. He hugged her back with all his might.

"So good to see you up and about," Celia said on her tiptoes, planting a loud kiss on his cheek. "What the hell were you doing in that room for so long?"

"I had to take a very cold shower," he said, throwing me a sly look and making me blush all over again.

My sister's eyes ping-ponged between Jem and me. "Are you guys getting it on finally?"

Oh God! My cheeks burned so hot, I thought I would burst into flames.

Jem chuckled. "Come on, Celia, you're making your sister blush," he said. "No, unfortunately we are not, as you said, getting it on. More like starting at a simmer."

I went to make coffee and hide in the kitchen while my two uncouth sidekicks chatted away in the living room. When I came back with a mug in each hand, they were laughing uncontrollably.

"What's so funny?" I asked, handing one of the mugs to Jem.

"Celia was telling me about the fiasco with the repellent you got from Marcy." Jem took the mug to his lips. For the hundredth time that day, my cheeks were set aflame.

"Really, Celia? You told him about that?" I was mortified.

Jem had that look, the one he always got when he knew he had something on me, something to hold over me. "And after all that, it didn't even work…." A little smirk appeared on his lips as he turned to my sister. "Tell me again, Celia; why didn't it work?"

Saint Helpful opened her round eyes and her mouth without a thought. "Because it would only work on someone she didn't love—"

"Okay, that's more than enough," I interrupted, holding my hand in front of her. "And you." I pointed at Jem. "Stop looking so smug. Marcy's magic doesn't work the way it's supposed to."

"It does, too!" *Shit, Celia! Just shut up for once.* My outraged little sister looked at me with accusing eyes. "Her stuff does work."

There was no winning with these people. I threw my arms up in the air and went back to the kitchen to get my own mug of coffee. I loved them, but there were times I wanted to strangle them.

Celia stayed for a few hours, until she had to go to work at the hospital. She gave Jem another bear hug, and I saw her whisper something in his ear. Then she hugged me. Twice. "I love you, sis," she said.

"I love you, too, crazy." She left while I waved good-bye from the door. For a moment I wondered where the undercover cops were, but then gave up. It didn't matter who or where they were as long as they did their job. I closed the door and looked at Jem, stretched on the couch and ready to watch TV.

"What did she tell you?" I asked, my arms crossed in front of my chest.

He smiled. "None of your business," he replied. "It's between your sister and me."

Huffing a little, I walked to my room. "I'm going to change and do some yoga. You guys stressed me out."

When I came back after changing into yoga pants and a T-shirt, Jem was waiting. "Ready?" Ready for what? "We're doing yoga, right?"

Apparently we were doing yoga together. I turned on the music, unrolled my mat, and sat on it. "Do as you please," I said, still a bit miffed at his refusal to tell me what my sister had told him.

From the corner of my eye I watched him as he meditated to the sound of the ocean waves and the barking of the seagulls. My belly tightened as, in spite of all the abuse his body had endured, he flowed from one pose to another with the power of a warrior and the grace of a dancer. I closed my eyes to bar images of him from my mind, but they kept coming. I was so screwed.

After *savasana,* I felt much more relaxed. As I was rolling my mat, I felt Jem's body heat next to mine. I turned around to face him and he wrapped his hands around my waist, pulling me closer until our bodies were touching. A wave of heat ran through me, from my toes to the top of my head, dissolving everything in between.

"In spite of everything, Emily Rose," he said, his warm voice caressing me, "I'm so glad this brought us close together again."

Oh God, give me strength.

He leaned forward a little and I thought he was going to kiss me, but his lips overshot mine and came to rest against my ear. "I love you, Emily Rose." Shivers ran through me as our skin made contact. "Always have and always will."

Dropping his hands, Jem turned around and went into his room, leaving me standing in the living room, shaking with yearning.

Damn you!

***

I spent the first couple hours of my sleep time tossing and turning until the sheets and blankets on my bed were rolled up like a sushi roll. I kicked them off the bed and sprang up into a sitting position. *Maybe a little yoga breathing will help.* In through the nose, out through the mouth, belly breathing, three-stage breathing, focused breathing…. Damn it! Just couldn't settle down. My mind was going a million miles per hour, and my senses were so alive my whole body was tingling with electric energy.

I got out of bed and tiptoed my way out of the room and into the kitchen. To my surprise, Jem was there, too. He didn't hear me come in at first, so I had a moment to admire the view. Still wearing the same joggers as before, hanging low on his hips, he now wore no shirt. His lean and yet muscular chest, stained still with bruises now starting to fade into a greenish shade, was bare in all its magnificence. I gulped.

I should just go back to bed.

Just as I was about to turn around and make a hasty retreat, Jem lifted his eyes and saw me. "Em. What are you doing up?"

With what I hoped was a nonchalant attitude, I took a step or two into my small kitchen. "I couldn't sleep." My voice shook. "You?"

He leaned against the counter and dragged a hand over his eyes. "Same here. Couldn't sleep. Warming up some milk. Want some? We can spike it with…." He looked around, searching for some alcoholic drink.

"Sorry," I said, giggling a little. "The only alcohol I have is a bottle of red and some antiseptic."

Pretending to be disappointed, Jem lifted his hands up in the air. "Oy vey!"

The movement of his arms had made the muscles tighten across his chest and his pants slide down his hips a couple more inches. I couldn't stop my mouth from dropping open with a tiny gasp. He threw me a rakish smile, and I made a childish face at him. Why did he bring out that side of me?

"Do you like what you see?"

Asshole!

"Don't be so full of yourself," I managed to say. "I was shocked at how dark your bruises still are." Nice save.

He chuckled, turning back to the stove. He poured us some warm milk and then handed me one of the mugs. I smiled. His mom had always given us hot milk when I slept over at his house as a child. "You'll sleep better," she would say. Funny how little things like that seemed to stick with us for the rest of our lives.

Making no effort to go sit somewhere, we stood there drinking our milk in silence, watching each other from beneath half-closed eyelids. Could he hear my heart? I would be surprised if he couldn't, because it was beating furiously in my chest. Something within me had liquefied and I didn't want to move for fear of turning into a puddle.

When he first took a step toward me, I almost jumped out of my skin. My pulse accelerated, and my fertile imagination came up with a million scenarios of what might be about to happen.

Putting down his mug, Jem took a few more steps until he was standing right in front of me, his full six-foot-two stature towering over my tiny frame. He took the mug from my hands, set it down on the counter, and leaned in until my body was wedged between the wall and his.

My heart was working its way up my throat when he bent down so his face was almost level with mine. Swoony was the only word I could come up with to describe what I felt when his intense blue eyes locked with mine. *Oh crap!* There was no way out of this now.

His lips descended on the side of my neck and worked their fluttery magic up and down my overly sensitive skin. With maddening slowness, he suckled on my earlobe until a moan of pleasure escaped my lips.

"Do you want me to stop?" he whispered in my ear, his warm breath setting my skin on fire.

I willed my lips to say *yes*, but all my senses betrayed me. I lifted my hands and crossed them behind his neck, drawing him closer. "Damn you, Jem," I said instead.

Our lips, hungry for each other's, met and melded. As his tongue danced its way to meet mine, his arms tightened around my waist, sliding under my T-shirt and flattening themselves on my back. Of its own accord, my body rubbed against his, craving more contact, more heat.

"Are you sure?" he asked against my mouth, his voice husky with desire.

Deprived of the power of speech, I took hold of his waistband and began pulling his pants down. It was his turn to moan.

His hands went to the lower edges of my T-shirt and he pulled it over my head, leaving me bare. There was such hunger in his eyes as they roamed over my breasts, the fire in my core flared into a full blast. Bending down, he covered my breast with his mouth. My concept of ecstasy was rewritten at that very moment. Years of frustrated yearning flooded my thoughts and my body, demanding release.

I arched against his mouth, wanting to be closer still. He lingered there, his warm tongue teasing me to the point of no return. My fingers were entwined in his curls, pressing his head against me, demanding in a way I had never been before.

When Jem came up for air, I started pulling on his joggers, desperately trying to feel all of him. My hands fumbled with the waistband. Jem let go of me for a second, long enough to pull down the offending pants and free me of mine right after.

Time stopped as we stood facing each other, naked and winded. I was in awe of the body that housed my best friend. Even covered in bruises and half-healed scars, he was a work of art. A masterpiece I wanted for myself alone. His eyes traveled and caressed the length of me, and I—normally so self-conscious of my flaws—melted beneath his scrutiny. His body trembled under my gaze, and I knew he liked what he saw.

In a smooth move, Jem picked me up in his arms and carried me to his bedroom as if I weighed nothing. It was a good thing he did, for I wasn't sure I would've been able to walk on my wobbly legs. I had waited so long for this moment that I was still not sure I wasn't dreaming. He gently laid me down on the bed and then slid over me, wringing a low groan of pleasure from me.

"Say you love me." Jem's voice surprised me out of my trance. His face was hovering over mine, his whole body stretched above me, a cocoon of heat and hardness. I looked up into the deep ocean of his eyes, drunk with desire, intoxicated by my feelings for him—physical and otherwise. "Tell me you love me. Please."

In a moment of clarity I wondered if it were possible that he didn't know. I had always assumed he knew I was in love with him and had been for most of our lives. But at that moment he seemed almost desperate to hear me say it, as if he needed validation.

"I've loved you since we were teens in high school, you fool," I said. "You're the one who didn't—"

Jem didn't let me finish. He kissed me, swallowing me whole—body and soul. "I did. I always did love you," he said, letting me go for a moment. "I loved you so much it scared the hell out of me."

Supporting himself on one arm, Jem brushed the other

hand from my throat down between my breasts and slid it between my thighs. I cried out and wrapped my leg around him, daring him to caress me deeper.

While his fingers were creating havoc with my senses, he turned his attention to my breasts again.

"Shit, Jem. I'm going to explode," I yelled.

His hard body slid against mine again, prying my legs apart. I could feel his heat against mine, and I lost it. My hands came around him, flattened themselves on his backside, and pushed him hard into me. We were finally one and it was heaven.

Chapter Thirteen

Healing Old Wounds

If the world came to an end at that exact moment, I wouldn't care. Lying in the arms of my best friend and the love of my life I was, without doubt, the happiest I had ever been, and even an apocalypse wouldn't be able to change that.

Jem's chest rose rhythmically, and his heart beat quietly against my ear. I couldn't stop touching him. As he slept, my hand explored every ridge of every muscle on his chest and abdomen, his strong arms, his beautiful face, his lips…. My lips soon followed my fingers and, before I knew it, I had straddled him and was replaying the most mortifying scene of my life. Only this time, I was sure he wouldn't call out another girl's name.

I reveled in the feel of him reacting to my touch even as he slept. Sliding my hands over his chest, I leaned over him and reached for his mouth. I traced his full, luscious lips, sighing happily when he moaned in response. I followed the caress with my lips, first nibbling and then parting them with my tongue. His arms came suddenly around me and, with a flip, he had me turned around and was now the one straddling me.

"You were awake all the time," I said with a pretend pout.

Jem, ocean-blue eyes wide open, laughed. "I wasn't sleeping back then, and I'm definitely not sleeping now." He crushed his lips against mine again, and I swooned. "I never thought of protection, Em," he whispered, his breath caressing my lips. "You know, a condom…?"

I giggled softly, my mouth still touching his. "I'm on the pill," I told him. "We're okay."

Teasingly, he nibbled on my lips inciting a whimper from me. "We're so much better than okay."

"I love you, Jeremy Peter," I said against his mouth, inhaling his breath. Dropping my hold on his waist, I slipped my hand down between us to touch him. His moan of pleasure made me smile and melt underneath him.

"You're killing me, girl," he said, his head bending backward as I stroked him again. "Holy shit!"

With a throaty grunt, he bent down to flick his tongue across my breasts and track kisses all along my lower belly, insinuating himself between my thighs in a maddening caress. A flow of energy and ecstasy ran through me. I arched against him, begging for more.

Just as an inexplicable surge of overwhelming feelings came over me, threatening to explode at any time, I heard a loud noise. At first I thought it was my heart beating, but then I realized it was someone knocking at the door. Jem lifted his head and we stared at each other, surprised.

What a time to come knocking! "Who could that be?" I asked, still throbbing with yearning. God, I wanted him to resume his loving. The knocking continued, more insistent this time. "Shit! I better go see who it is."

As I made to move out of the bed, Jem grabbed one of my legs. "Don't go!" He ran a finger along my inner thigh. I shivered.

Whoever was at the door knocked again. I sighed. "Got to go," I said as I reluctantly slid off the bed and away from him.

While I hastily slipped into a pair of his sweats—I had left mine in the kitchen—and a T-shirt, he lay on the bed, magnificent in his birthday suit, watching my every move. My heart clenched inside my chest. Was it possible I loved him even more now?

Closing the door behind me, I left the room to go answer the front door. I looked through the peephole and grunted when my eyes met a bright red head on the other side. Marcy!

"What are you doing here?" I asked her, trying not to sound too annoyed. She stood in the doorway looking strangely impressive in one of her outlandish outfits.

"I had a vision," she said, sashaying her way into the house. Her sun-yellow ruffled skirt bounced around her as she moved. "I had to come and tell you."

My heart fell. Not again! I still didn't believe in her "visions," but she seemed to have a knack of having them right before something bad happened.

"What now?" I asked, dropping to the couch in defeat.

Her bright hair was decorated with a giant blue bow. "What were you doing?" she asked, shrewd eyes studying me.

"Where's Jem?"

"He's still asleep," I answered quickly, suddenly conscious of the fact I wasn't wearing any underwear. "What's going on, Marcy?"

She waved a long finger in the air. "No, no. You can't get away that easy." She looked around, her gaze zooming in on the kitchen. "Your clothes are on the floor in the kitchen."

Shit! She had eyes like a hawk. "I was too lazy to pick them up when I went to bed last night," I lied. Couldn't I have come up with a better explanation? That sounded lame even to me.

"Jem's pants are right next to yours." It was a statement of fact, not a question. "You guys… did it, didn't you?"

I sprang to my feet. "Oh for God's sake, Marcy," I exclaimed. "It's none of your business anyway."

As if on cue, Jem showed up wearing another pair of joggers but no shirt, his hair disheveled and his feet bare. My insides turned to mush again.

"Hey, Marcy! What are you doing here so early?" he asked, coming next to me and putting his arm around my shoulders. Well, the cat was out of the bag.

The little witch smiled, genuinely pleased to confirm Jem and I were an item now. "Finally!" she said, clapping her hands. "So happy for you guys!"

My cheeks were burning. "Why are you here?" I asked again, more to hide my embarrassment than out of real curiosity.

"Oh yeah, my vision." Snapping out of her daze, Marcy straightened her little black T-shirt. "I had a vision that something big is about to happen."

Never a good sign coming from her. I squirmed against Jem. "What do you mean *big*?"

"Not sure." She sat down on the couch. Her pink stiletto heels had to be killing her. "Not necessarily bad, but big, life-changing even."

That was helpful. I held back my eyeroll.

It was Jem who defused the awkward situation and prevented me from saying something I would regret later. "Coffee, anyone?"

Both Marcy and I nodded enthusiastically, and Jem turned around to go make coffee. I watched him as he moved, my eyes glued to his sexy behind, heat climbing up my neck all the way to the roots of my hair. Marcy was looking at me from the corner of her eye, an amused smile on her lips.

"He is yummy," she said. "You have very good taste." That struck me as funny and I burst out laughing. "What's so funny?"

The doorbell rang. *More visitors? What is this, Grand Central Station?* Marcy got up and ran to the door before I could even react. From the door I heard the familiar voice of my sister. They whispered a few words, and then I heard a high screech.

"Oh my God, oh my God!" Celia said as she hopped into the house in my direction. "Is it true? You and Jem are together?"

Hell no! Not Celia as well. I felt as if time had turned back to my middle school days. With a roll of my eyes, I braced myself for the hug that was surely coming. But it never did.

Instead, my sister had run into the kitchen and straight into the arms of my love.

"I'm so happy for you guys," she was saying as she half strangled poor Jem.

"You're choking me, girl," he said, his chuckle belying his complaint. "You're not any happier than I am."

Still hanging from his neck, Celia giggled. "Don't be so sure. We're going to be in-laws."

"Emily Rose," he called out to me. "Your sister is marrying us off already."

I laughed. It was impossible not to, surrounded by crazy people. "Watch out! Next she'll be making plans for our firstborn."

Jem made a horrified face and managed to free himself from my sister's iron grip. "I need to be with my girl." He leapt over the back of the couch and dropped beside me. "Missed you," he whispered in my ear.

Smiling like a fool, I laid my head on his shoulder. "You were in the kitchen for less than five minutes," I said, giggling.

He brushed his lips on mine. "Let's get rid of these girls. I have plans for the two of us in that great big bed of yours." Tingling replaced all other feeling along my skin.

Celia sat down next to us. "I heard that. We're not going anywhere," she said with a frown. "Marcy is sure there is something major about to happen, and I am not going to let you guys be kidnapped again."

Jem laughed out loud. "What are you going to do? Annoy the kidnappers to death?"

She looked outraged, a hand lying flat on her chest. "I have skills!"

It was my turn to laugh. "You sure do, sis," I said, letting go of Jem to hug her. "You have some serious skills."

Marcy was standing by the kitchen, coffee mug in hand. "Coffee is really not my thing," she said when we all looked at her.

"What is this all about, Marcy?" I asked, holding my sister's hand.

Marcy, teetering on her pink stilettos, sniffed the coffee in her hands. "Not quite sure." She frowned. "It's fuzzy."

"Come on, red witch," Jem said. I liked the new nickname. It fit her to a tee. "You have to give us something."

With the mug still in her hands, Marcy took a few steps toward the middle of the room. "I just sense something is about to change."

Jem and I exchanged a look. Something had just changed. And it was a good change. Marcy noticed our silent exchange. "Not *that*!" She waved her hand, nearly spilling the coffee. "Something coming from outside."

We all looked at the window. "Like *outside*, outside?" Celia asked.

"No. More like outside the inner group," she said, finally putting the mug down on the coffee table and perching on one of the couch arms. "From an outside entity."

The phone rang interrupting the silence that followed Marcy's ominous statement. I jumped to go get it from the kitchen counter where I had left it. A quick glance at the caller ID told me it was Detective Jarvas. Uh-oh, a call from him right after hearing about a witch's vision didn't bode well.

"Hello, sweetheart." I loved the way he addressed me. It

was like somewhere down the line he had adopted me as his surrogate daughter. "I have big news."

I chanced a glance at Jem, who along with the other two were staring at me nervously. "Yes?"

"Tina will be testifying tomorrow," he said, pausing to cough. "Sorry. Damn cigarettes! She's arriving from Paris today and tomorrow she'll be in court. We need you guys there, as well. I'll have a couple of my guys pick you up tomorrow at seven."

"Is this a good thing?" I asked. Jem was mouthing a question I couldn't answer yet.

"It's a very good thing," he said, a smile in his voice. "Once she testifies, you guys won't be in danger anymore. You can go back to your normal lives."

Would that be such a good thing? As much as I missed my little students and my trips to yoga and the coffee shop, I was having a little too much fun in the confinement of my own house.

"Thank you, Detective," I said. "I truly appreciate all you've done for us. I guess we'll see you tomorrow?"

"I'll be there with bells on. See you tomorrow." He hung up, and I held the phone to my ear for a few more seconds.

When I turned around, three pairs of eyes were fixed on me. "Well?" Jem voiced the question in everybody's minds.

"Tina will be testifying tomorrow," I announced, realizing her name still tasted sour in my mouth. "Our jail time is almost over."

My voice must have shown some of the trepidation I felt about going back to our so-called normal lives, because Jem sprang to his feet and strode across to hold me. "I kind of like our prison," he said, kissing me on the forehead so tenderly I melted into a boneless mass in his arms. "You're going to let me sleep over a little longer, aren't you?" He had a wicked sparkle in his eyes.

Forgetting my sister and Marcy, I tilted my head up, swung my arms around his neck, and kissed him full on the lips. I could hear the girls sucking in their breaths and then a whispered "aww" followed by "That's so sweet." I quit listening because the flapping of angel wings in my ears was too loud to allow any other sounds to come through.

***

Tina's testimony was short and sweet, if a little anticlimactic. After all we had to go through, it seemed like there ought to be a little more pizazz to the whole proceedings. However, everything was over and done in less than an hour. We filed out of the courtroom and sat on a bench outside, waiting to talk to Detective Jarvas and one of the prosecutors for some housekeeping tidy up. Jem, handsome in a well-cut suit, had his hand over my shoulders while we quietly talked.

"Aww, isn't that sweet," we heard. Our heads snapped up to find Tina, with her astonishing dark looks, smirking at us, her voice dripping bitchiness. "You finally got what you deserve, Jeremy."

As if by mutual accord, we both stood. There was no way this incredibly gorgeous woman was going to look down on me, literally or figuratively.

"What exactly do you mean, Tina?" I asked, my hand flat on Jem's chest. I could feel his muscles coiled and ready to spring into action.

"He was always such a baby," Tina said, her eyes roving Jem's body with despisement. "Always missing his mommy and daddy. And his best friend, Emily Rose. Oh, what was he going to do without her? He drove me up the walls with the whining. Not even his pitiful lovemaking could make up for what I had to endure."

My hand stopped Jem from moving forward. "You're just bitter he left you as soon as he could," I said, my heart bleeding at her words. A little for Jem, but also for myself as she reminded me that they did indeed have a sexual relationship at some point.

"Oh honey," she said, her Italian ancestry coming out in her voice and gestures. "You can keep him. He wasn't that good in bed anyway."

Okay, I'm not the violent kind. Hell, I'm not even the reacting kind. I'm the girl who never posts back on Facebook if someone says something nasty, and who goes out of her way not to argue with anyone about anything. But Tina had me really hot under the collar.

I stepped forward, grabbed her by her scarf—her shirt had such a low cut there was nothing else for me to hold on to—and, rising on my tiptoes, got in her face. "You listen to me, bitch." I emphasized the last word for flavor. "Jem almost died because he was kind enough to volunteer to be your companion in this adventure of yours. He. Almost. Freaking. Died. Do you understand that, you dim-witted bitch? You should be thanking him, but instead you're very happy to put him down. Sour grapes, that's all it is. You better apologize, or I'm going to throttle you right in the middle of this hallway."

I must have sounded dead serious because, in spite of my tiny five-foot-two compared to her five-eight, she took a step backward, visibly shaken.

"All right, all right," she said, her hands up in front of her. "Don't get your panties all in a twist. Jeremy, I'm sorry."

She didn't sound sorry at all, but I figured that was the best we were going to get from her, and I let her go. "Now don't you ever bother us again," I added for effect. I watched as she walked away in a huff, her too-perfect butt moving from one side to the other, and her heels click-clacking on the marble floor.

I turned to Jem, who, I belatedly realized, was too quiet. His deep ocean eyes were clouded over and his jaw was clenched.

"I'm sorry, Emily Rose," he said in a quiet voice, his arms dropped alongside his body.

"What are you sorry for?" I asked, a little bitterness in my voice.

"Everything." He swallowed hard. "Taking off to France with Tina, sleeping with her… fuck! Sleeping with all the other women I slept with so I didn't have to face my feelings for you. I wish I could erase all of it, but I can't."

My heart was conflicted, but I was sure of one thing. "I'm not saying it doesn't hurt me to think about it, but all that matters is now," I said. "And *now* I love you and you love me. We're together after all these years of fighting a losing war."

I managed a little smile. "Let's not spend any time regretting what it was, and just enjoy what we have."

Hesitantly at first, he opened his arms and took a step toward me. There was no such hesitation from me. I was craving the contact, the safety his arms offered me. I wanted to linger there forever and forget the last five years—leave it all behind. As his warm lips latched on to mine I wondered for a brief moment how I had survived that long without it.

"I love you, Emily Rose," he whispered into my hair as he bent down to cocoon me with his body. "I love you so much it scares me."

"That's because she's a scary one," my sister's voice butted in.

We both let go a little and looked at Celia, who had just arrived from her shift in the hospital. Sporting her scrubs and funky-looking Crocs, my sister smiled huge. "So good to see you guys all lovey-dovey."

Typically, she threw herself into the middle of our hug. "Group hug!" she yelled, her voice muffled by Jem's and my bodies.

"Can I join?" It was the good detective, his nicotine-yellowed fingers wiggling in the air.

We all laughed and pulled ourselves apart. The courthouse was getting very crowded, so we decided to go sit in a nearby coffeehouse and talk for a while. I so wanted to thank Jarvas for all the protection and support he had given us throughout this whole ordeal.

After we had settled into a nice, private booth and ordered our drinks, we sat back to finally relax for a while. It had been an intense few weeks, to say the least.

Detective Jarvas bent slightly over the table and looked Jem in the eye. "So, I've talked to a few people in the department and I managed to find you the best therapist money can buy," he said. Surprise made me snap my head up. What was he talking about? "Since you were in some way screwed by the system, the department is willing to waive the fees. Dr. Lehy works with cops who have gone through some traumatic experiences."

"Wait a minute," I said, my hand shooting up. "What the hell are you talking about?"

Jem was the one who explained. "I've been having trouble, so the detective offered to find me some help." He looked almost apologetic. "Sorry I didn't tell you."

"No need to apologize." I held his hand. "I'm glad you did. I was worried." I turned to the policeman. "Thank you so much, Detective. For everything."

Jarvas shook his head and smiled. "Which leads me to the next question," he said, his eyebrows arching up. "What was that kiss in the court hallway all about?"

I must have turned beet red, but Jem just laughed, slid an arm over my shoulders, and pulled me to him. "Just a demonstration of what we will be doing—a lot—in the foreseeable future." And his luscious lips met mine again.

Chapter Fourteen

Mended Hearts

This could not be happening. I tried to wiggle off the blindfold that covered my eyes, but my hands, tied behind my back, didn't cooperate. I could feel Jem beside me doing the same thing, and I drew some comfort from the heat of his body being thrown against mine every time the car negotiated a curve.

"This is ridiculous," I yelled, raving mad. "Let us go."

"Shut up or I will gag you," the voice said from the front seat. "It was bad enough I had to tie your hands to stop you from messing with your blindfolds. Don't make it any more difficult." I growled under my breath and, giving up trying to free myself, sat back against Jem's side.

"Are you okay?" I whispered. He had been going to therapy now for a week or so, but I still worried he wasn't doing well.

"Never better," he said. Was he being sarcastic, or did he mean it? It was hard to tell without looking into his face as he said it. Body language was all-important.

"Well, I'm sick of this," I said, unable to contain my irritation. I got another warning from the front seat.

The car stopped finally, and I heard doors open and close and then open again.

"All right, get out," we heard. "We're here."

We were pulled out of the car and our hands untied. When I finally was able to remove the blindfold, I couldn't believe what I was seeing. It didn't seem to belong there—a small, toasted-yellow cottage in the middle of the woods.

"What is this place? Hansel and Gretel's cottage?" I asked to hide my shock.

Celia came behind me to untie the black scarf she had used for a blindfold, now hanging from my neck. "Do you like it?" she asked.

Like was not remotely a good word to describe what I felt at that moment. The cottage was adorable, straight out of a fairy tale or a travel brochure. The woods where it hid from modern life were gorgeous and lush. "How did you find this place?"

"A friend of my mom bought it some years ago. She uses it for retreats with her writer friends," Marcy replied, her bright red lips in stark contrast with her ivory skin. "I asked if I could use it for a good cause, and when I told her your story, she gave me the keys."

Jem shook his head and looked at me. "What story did you tell her exactly?" he asked.

"You know, your love story." She looked so innocent; if I hadn't known better I would've believed her. I gave her a piercing look. "All right. I also told her about the kidnappings and all. You may end up in one of her books."

Celia stepped in. "The point is that we wanted to give you both a couple days away from all the madness." She laid her head on my shoulder. "Time for you guys to reconnect and…." Her naughty smile was back on. "Maybe make me a nephew or niece?"

I slapped the back of her head. "Knucklehead! We just got back together and you're already making baby shower plans?"

"Help me, Jem," she cried, running into his arms. Laughing, he welcomed her into a bear hug. "He's so much nicer than you, Emily."

We all went inside and I was in awe of how beautifully simple the cottage was, with its sparse vintage furniture, fresh flowers in every corner, and lacy curtains in every window. It was as if we had stepped into a different world.

"We're going to leave you now," Celia announced after we all had shared a nice cup of coffee.

"You're taking the car?" I asked, a little worried about being left without transportation.

"Of course. We can't very well walk home, can we?" my smart-aleck sister said.

I crossed my arms in what Celia liked to call my "teacher's stance." "Marcy is a witch. Can't you just fly out on her broom?"

Celia cackled like a true witch. "Very funny. We will leave you here carless so you can really connect. You have a phone for emergencies." She waved at us and grabbed her purse to leave. "We're just a half hour out."

Jem frowned. "But it took over an hour to get here," he said, leaning against my back. My insides turned to liquid.

Marcy had also picked up her gigantic purse. "That's because we drove around to make it seem farther than it is," she explained, handing me the house keys. "Let's go, Celia. Let the lovebirds roost."

The girls drove away as we watched them from the beautiful little front step. As soon as they had vanished around the bend, Jem pulled me to him and nuzzled my neck. Tiny bursts of electricity went through me as his lips touched my skin, and his fingers crawled slowly underneath my shirt.

"I don't know about you, but I think we've earned this," he said in my ear.

We so had earned this. When we were younger I used to say that life with Jem was an adventure. He had sure proved me right for the last few weeks.

"Are you hungry?" I asked, suddenly shy. Until this moment we had been around other people. There were the cops at first, then friends and family. Never a true moment alone. Here we were truly on our own, just Jem and me.

My best friend's blue eyes latched on mine. "I am famished." His voice had dropped to a sexy whisper. "But not for food."

Before I could respond, he pulled his T-shirt over his head and threw it into one of the bushes lining the small driveway. My heart began beating like a drum, deafening me. The color of his chest looked a lot more normal than it had in a while, but streaks of yellowish bruises still crossed his pectoral and abdominal muscles, and some of the wounds had begun to heal into angry reddish scars.

I reached out to touch them. Jem followed my fingers with his eyes, allowing me to explore the damaged skin, shivering a little in the cool air. He then stripped me of my shirt. With a big aerial arch, it dropped on another nearby bush. I couldn't move because my legs had turned to mush. With a little flourish, Jem turned me around and I felt his fingers on my back. Deftly he unhooked my bra, slid it off my arms, and dropped it on the ground. I felt the crisp air caress my bare breasts and shivered with excitement.

Jem stepped closer, until his chest was touching my back. His hands skated around my ribs to cup my breasts. A moan escaped me as his lips nibbled on my ear, and his hands performed their magic. In a moment of hysterical confusion, I was in awe at how well my breasts fit in his hands. We did fit well together, as if we had been made for each other.

Turning me around again, Jem crushed his lips on mine, and the world ceased to exist. I lost myself in the taste of him, the warmth of his tongue playing with mine, the rousing feel of his fingers on my back. "Let's go inside," he said against my lips. "I want to strip you of every piece of clothing and every lingering doubt you may still have about my love."

We stumbled against the door and then into the house, all the way to the bedroom across the small hallway. My hands had taken on a life of their own and latched on to the waistband of his pants, struggling with the button.

"Damn! I can't unbutton this," I exclaimed, frustrated.

Jem laughed and came to my rescue. In a fraction of a moment we were standing in the center of the room watching each other strip. I would never get tired of looking at my Jem. I loved watching him as a teenager, and I loved it even better as an adult. This time I made the first move. I stepped forward and brushed my hands from his collarbone, all the way down his chest, his belly muscles, and lower. He groaned and moved closer. I could feel him respond, and I trembled in anticipation.

I squealed a little in surprise and delight when he swooped me off the floor to carry me to the bed. Jem lowered me gently onto it and then slid along my body, tantalizingly slow. His skin rubbing against mine made me quiver like a leaf in the summer breeze. I wrapped my legs around him, an urgent need to have him inside of me taking over.

With my hands pressing and guiding him, I made him perfectly aware of my intentions. He moaned into my neck, and with a thrust we became one. I swear I saw and heard fireworks. It was both a thrill ride and the most relaxing, soothing thing I had ever felt. We belonged together. If I had had any doubts before that moment, I had none left now.

We moved together in a sensual dance, a crescendo of sensation leading to an epic explosion. Breathless and sated, we held each other for a while, not wanting to break our bond. I kissed him, stroking his lips with my tongue until he responded in kind.

"I love you," I said, against his lips. "Why didn't we do this a long time ago?"

Jem nibbled on my lower lip. "Because young people are dumb," he said with a chuckle. "I was definitely seriously dumb. Dumber than a doorknob."

The room had gotten darker, and I realized night was falling. I rolled the two of us so I was now on top of him, straddling him and with my hands flat on his scarred chest. "A very hot dummy," I said, my hands gently exploring each scar, each fading bruise. "I still get mad when I see these."

A sad smile erupted on his lips. "It will be okay," he whispered, not offering anything else.

"We never talked about it," I ventured, chancing a glance at him. "I was very scared, Jem. For me, but especially for you. After I saw what they did to you, I knew they would keep on doing it until they killed you." My voice had taken on a desperate tone.

As if by mutual agreement, we sat up, leaning against the headboard side by side, my head resting on his shoulder, his hand casually lying on my thigh. "I was scared, too, Emily Rose," he finally said. "I put up a strong face—what I had left of one, anyway—but inside I was terrified. I still have nightmares, but the therapist has really helped me deal with it."

I pulled him closer against my side, my hand sliding across his waist to curl around his other hip. "It must have been horrifying. I can't even imagine."

"The pain was brutal but...." He paused, looking for the right words to express his feelings. "It was the feeling of helplessness that really got me. When you're being beaten to a pulp and you can't do anything about it... you just feel hopeless and helpless. And then later, you hate yourself because you were weak."

My head popped up to look into his eyes. "You were not

weak, Jem. There were two of them—giants, they were—and only one of you."

Jem hung his head a little. "I know, but you still feel weak. You wonder if maybe there was something you could have done to prevent it, to fight back."

It was the first time he'd been willing to talk about it with me. I realized that it was a big moment, a defining moment in our relationship.

"And I was so scared they were going to hurt you," he continued, caressing my cheek. "They threatened to do all kinds of things to you if I wouldn't cooperate. I couldn't cooperate because I knew nothing, but they wouldn't believe me. They just wouldn't believe me."

He was shaking against me. I pulled the sheets and blankets over us even though I knew he wasn't shivering from the cold. "It's over, Jem."

A broad smile stretched across his lips. "It is. And I have you now," he said. "It was all worth it in the end."

"You know." I brushed a finger across his chest. "You didn't have to get pulverized to get me. You had me at *hello again*." I batted my eyelashes in a poor imitation of the classic Hollywood starlets. He laughed.

"What are you talking about? You almost killed me with your laser looks when we met at the coffee shop," he said, a finger tilting my chin up slightly. "You do have the most delicious lips I have ever tasted." As if to demonstrate what he meant, Jem lowered his lips to mine in a long, leisurely kiss.

A hot tingle coursed through my body. "Shit. You've got to stop doing that to me," I said when we pulled apart, his deep ocean eyes burrowing into my soul.

"Doing what?" Jem asked as his hand brushed its way down to my breast.

"That!" I uttered, breathless. "That thing you do with your lips, and your hands… and your eyes. Shit, Jem. I'm so in love with you." Totally, 100 percent, overwhelmingly in love with my best friend.

Chapter Fifteen

Love and Confetti

"I don't need that, Marcy," I said, raising my voice to a level I normally used when my students were getting too loud. "I'm fine. Jem is fine."

My little witch friend was standing in front of me, her hand on her hip, looking as eccentric as always. A small green vial peeked through her fingers, her hand extended toward me. "But you guys went through so much. You need something to help you get over it."

"I'm fine, Marcy. I really am." I brushed my hand over my face. "And Jem is seeing a therapist. We don't need another potion."

Marcy didn't seem convinced. Her hair, redder than usual—or maybe it was just the way the light was hitting it—glowed like a flame, and her teeth bit the corner of her lips.

"It won't hurt to try it," she said. I was not so sure. Marcy's potions, even though surprisingly effective, were also a bit on the weird side. I hated to admit I was a little scared of them. She stretched her hand in my direction, trying to hand me the vial.

I grabbed it with a sigh. "Okay, I'll take it. But I'm not promising anything." She smiled at me with a look that told me she just knew I was going to swallow that green goo. I hated when people seemed to know me better than I did. "Is Celia coming?"

We were sitting in our usual booth in the coffee house. Jem was on one of his visits to the therapist and Celia was missing in action. I'd thought she was coming with her witch friend, but she never showed up.

"She said she would meet us here," Marcy said, her polka-dot bow sliding a little down her forehead. She raised her hand to adjust it. "How does it feel to be back at work?"

The scent of the coffee in my hands was comforting. "Weird," I confessed. "But the kids seemed happy to see me. They have been well-behaved beyond my expectations. I think they missed me." I giggled, remembering how shocked I had been at the unusual good behavior coming from my fifth graders. With spring now in full bloom, what I liked to call the hormonal kick normally started to drive every fifth grade teacher insane. However, my students seemed immune to it this year. I was fully expecting the madness to start at any time.

Marcy smoothed some imaginary wrinkles of her bright pink blouse. "And how are things with the hot one?" Never one to mince words.

"Everything is going well," I said. *And none of your*

business, missy. "Are you seeing anybody?" I was curious. I had never seen her with any males. She was pretty in her own quirky way, and it was surprising she didn't seem to have a love interest. "I have never seen you with anybody."

"I haven't dated in a while," she said, staring at her bright pink nails. "I go on dates, but I'm not actually dating anyone. Why? Do you know someone as hot as Jem?"

I ignored the comment and took another sip. "I think you should try and find someone to share your life with." *That way, maybe you'll stay out of other people's affairs.* "Ever heard of online dating?"

"Too many creeps out there."

I couldn't find fault on that. I would so not date online, but so many people did it with great success. Or so they told me.

"Well, my two favorite girls in the world," Celia said, popping around the booth suddenly. She seemed chirpier than usual, and that just raised all my red flags. "Move over, red rover."

With a little shuffle of my bottom half, I made room for her in the booth. "Why are you so happy? Got a promotion or something?" It was the *something* that really worried me. Always the schemer, Celia was not to be trusted.

"It's sunny outside." It was not. "And life is great. Why shouldn't I be happy?"

"Because normally at this time of day—right between meals, and after a night shift at the hospital—you are crankier than an ornery old man." Lack of food and sleep always sent my sister into the pits of crankiness. When we were kids, I always kept some snacks around just in case.

"Not true! I'm just high on life. My sister is safe and in love with my friend. All is well with the world." Celia had this beatific expression that didn't go with her personality. I laughed. "What's so funny?"

"All you need is a halo and we'll have St. Celia drinking coffee with us," I said, choking on my coffee. "See what you do to me?"

With nowhere special to go and in good company, we talked for a while and slurped down coffee drinks like they were going out of style. Thankfully, caffeine did not affect me as it did most people, so I could drink quite a large amount of coffee without acting like Daffy Duck on amphetamines.

When Jem joined us an hour later, I was more than ready to move on to a different venue. We had made plans to go to yoga, Jem and I, an activity his therapist was 100 percent in support of. The art of stillness was very good for his restless soul.

Bags in hand, we said good-bye to Celia and Marcy, promising to meet them later for burgers at a local diner, and we walked down the street to the studio.

"I still have to change," I said, my fingers interlaced with his. His calloused skin against mine gave me familiar chills. Familiar was good. Familiar was just what I always wanted.

"I can help you with that," he said, a wicked glint in his eye. I laughed. "Really, I would love to help you change. We can lock the door in the dressing room and—"

"No way," I said vehemently while a very small part of me perked up at the idea. "Not kinky that way."

It was his turn to laugh. He stopped, turned around, and

drew me into his arms in a hug. "I know. That's my Emily Rose, whom I love. Don't ever change for anyone." He nuzzled the skin behind my ear.

"Not even for you? I bet you dream of doing many of those kinky… things," I said, heat rising to my cheeks.

"You can't even say it." He pulled me back so he could look me in the eye. "Kinky sex, you mean. And no, not even for me. I like the way we do it. No need for anything else."

The yoga class was relaxing and reinvigorating. When we left, I was feeling heavenly, as if my feet were floating above ground and the world had suddenly turned a wonderful shade of blue. Walking with Jem's hand across my shoulders had a lot to do with that feeling.

Celia and Marcy were already waiting for us at the small restaurant, big goblets of red wine in their hands. My eyebrow rose a little. My sister very rarely drank, and when she did it was either because she was too stressed about something—which she wasn't—or something big had happened that required celebrating.

"Wine?" I said, sitting on the chair Jem had pulled out for me. He sat right next to me and looked at the two girls with curiosity. "What's going on? First all the undue chirpiness and now wine? Something is going on. Dish, Celia."

"Why, a girl can't have a nice cup of wine without having something big to share?" she said, feigning outrage. Marcy almost choked on her wine. She knew something.

"Drop the act," I said, leaning over the table and placing my hand over my sister's. "What's going on?"

Celia and Marcy exchanged a look pregnant with meaning.

What are the two of them up to now?

"Remember that nice cop who was one of your watchers in the cabin in the woods?" she asked, putting the glass down.

"The one who got shot." My stomach churned at the image that popped into my head. Jem gave my thigh a squeeze under the table. "Of course I remember. How could I ever forget?"

There was another look exchanged between the two crazy ones. "Well, I'm glad to inform you that he is doing very well," she said, dabbing the corners of her mouth with a napkin. "He has fully recovered from his injuries and he is back at work with the police. Just a desk job for now. They don't want to push him yet."

I snorted a little. "I know that. Detective Jarvas has been keeping me informed of their recovery." He knew well that I felt responsible for their injuries and tried his best to put my mind at ease. Jem had confided that he often met one or both of the officers at the waiting room of his therapist.

Celia frowned, a funny little frown that made her look like an angry elf. "Well, excuse me for not knowing," she said. Then she smiled again. "That's not the news."

A pause for effect followed her words. Celia had always enjoyed a bit of drama. I smiled in spite of my annoyance.

"While he was at the hospital recovering I got to meet him," she continued, waving at a waiter. "We really should order dinner. I'm starved."

Impatiently, I looked at the menu and picked the first thing I saw. Jem, as if in cahoots with Celia to keep me in the dark as long as humanly possible, took his time reading the menu. In the end, he ordered a cheeseburger and cheese fries. I don't think he noticed the glare I threw at him.

The waiter, carrying the little notepad with our orders, walked away, and I looked pointedly at my sister. "Well?"

"Yes, so not only did I meet him, but I was assigned to his ward and was there for most of his hospital stay," she said, taking another sip of the wine. Could she go any slower? "To make a long story short"—*too late for that*—"we're dating."

If I had not been sitting, I would have fallen. I couldn't remember the last time my sister dated. Like Marcy, she went on dates but she had never seen the same guy twice. "You guys are dating? You mean really dating, like going-out-together-and-maybe-thinking-of-something-for-the-future dating?" I sounded like a blabbing idiot.

Celia nodded enthusiastically. "Yes, isn't that great?" she said. "Out of all that horrible drama, something beautiful happened."

Jem laughed heartily. "Sure. Because the fact that Emily Rose and I are finally together doesn't really count," he said.

Chagrin showed up on my baby sister's face. "Of course it counts." She bounced her eyes from Jem to me like a ping-pong ball. "I didn't mean it that way."

Giggling, I covered her hand with mine again. "I know that. Jem knows that," I said. "He's just messing with you." Jem nodded, an impish smile hovering on his lips.

Celia sighed loudly. "Oh thank God," she said, her body deflating like a balloon. "I don't want you to think I took advantage of your situation to get myself a man."

It was Marcy who jumped in. "Of course no one thinks that," she said. "But it is a happy coincidence. Don't you think so, Em?"

I stood up and walked around the table to hug my sister. "My baby sister's in love," I said, putting my arms around her and leaning into her back. "That's awesome."

"Maybe we could have a double wedding," Celia said. I dropped my arms and sat back down. "What?"

"Stop marrying us off," I said. "We just got back together and you already have all these plans for the rest of our lives."

Jem slid an arm over my shoulders and pulled me toward him. "What? Are you saying you wouldn't consider marrying me?"

I must have blushed furiously because the heat on my face was unbearable. "I didn't say that," I said. "It's just too soon to assume that's what's going to happen."

"Oh, it'll happen," Marcy declared unexpectedly. "It's in the cards, trust me."

We all stared at her. The little witch had her eyes half-closed and a huge red stain on the corner of her mouth. She was obviously pretty tipsy. As if by silent agreement, we all burst out laughing. Marcy looked at us with a question in her eyes, and we laughed even harder.

By the time the waiter came with our food, we had already forgotten the whole issue of marriage.

Or at least, that's what I wanted them all to believe.

***

"Ms. Lambert, can I go to the bathroom?" The strident little voice snapped me out of my reverie. Jeannie's small hand was stuck all the way up in the air, waving frantically like a small, fleshy flag. "Please. I really have to go now."

Unable to use my voice at that moment, I waved her my permission, and the child took off at great speed toward the classroom door. A few of the boys laughed out loud, and I'm certain one of them said something very rude. My head, stuck in the clouds, did not allow me to react. Let them fight amongst themselves. As long as there was no blood, everything was okay.

Coming back to work proved to be a lot harder than I thought. At first, I had been anxious to go back to the normal life—or, as I liked to call it now, pre-kidnapping life. However, I soon discovered that I couldn't go back. Not really. The truth was my life had changed dramatically, whether I liked to admit it or not. Nothing was like before.

Dave was no longer part of my life, and I was not sad about it at all. Instead, Jem now had the lead role in the movie script my life seemed to be following these days. I couldn't be happier. In spite of all the danger and trauma, I was exactly where I wanted to be. Jem was still suffering from bouts of PTSD, but all in all we had regained control of our lives—as much as anyone can ever claim to have.

"Ms. Lambert, you were in la-la land again," José said, his slanted black eyes squinting at me. I laughed. I used that line on them all the time. Now it was their turn to use it on me.

Being back at work had been a little challenging. I found myself daydreaming all the time and, more often than not, my fifth graders had to wake me up from my sleepwalking to demand being taught. I had Jem in my heart and in my brain.

Our relationship was like a storm that gathered power with every step. All I had to do was think about him, his beautiful blue eyes twinkling with mischief, and I was undone. Damn! Was he learning to use magic from Marcy?

"I'm sorry, class." I cleared my throat. "I'm a little absentminded today. Let's go back to the reading on the board. After the first read, what have you noticed about it?"

An ocean of waving hands swam in front of me. I smiled. I could bet half of them would not have a single thing to say if I called on them.

The day crawled painfully slowly, and by two in the afternoon I was ready to give up and suggest we all take a nap. A knock on the door interrupted my near-comatose state. Had I locked the door by mistake?

The door cracked open and, to my surprise, a huge bouquet of red roses slipped through the crack. My students gasped.

When a familiar face followed the flowers, my heart went all aflutter. Jem! I couldn't move as he walked inside the classroom, his hands clutching the bouquet and a big, stunning smile on his lips.

"Sorry to interrupt, guys," he said, waving at the students. "I have something very important to ask your teacher. Can I?"

For once, my hormonal young charges did not snicker. They all quietly nodded their assent, and feisty Giselle even waved him in.

"Wow!" Jem advanced into the classroom while surveying his surroundings. "What a great classroom you guys have here. You must have an awesome teacher."

The idiot was smiling and winking at all the kids. The girls had this rosy-cheeked, dreamy expression on their faces. Jem was working his male magic on all of them. As for the boys, they seemed just as entranced by the magnificent male with muscled biceps sticking out from his T-shirt.

He stopped in front of me by the Smartboard, and the smile turned into a full-fledged boyish grin. Heat crawled up my neck to my cheeks.

"Ms. Lambert," he said, winking. "Lovelier a creature have I rarely seen." The children giggled softly at his choice of words. He turned to them. "What do you think? Should I ask her?" The students all nodded emphatically, even though I doubt they knew what he meant. I didn't either.

"Jem," I lowered my voice. "What are you doing here?"

"Well, sweetheart, it's like this." He dropped to one knee, and all the girls gasped. I probably did, too. "I came to ask my best friend if she will marry me." He handed the bouquet to me.

I heard the sound of trotting hooves and I realized it was my heart. Accepting the bouquet from his hands, I tried to talk but couldn't.

"Marry him, Ms. Lambert," one of the girls yelled. "He's cute."

As if guessing my thoughts, another child came and took the flowers off my hands so I could hold Jem's. I still couldn't talk.

"I think she's in shock," said Max, the class smarty-pants. I laughed, the wetness of tears on the edge of my vision. Happy tears.

"I hate to say this, Em," Jem said, still on one knee, "but my knee hasn't been the same since it was kicked a few times. Are you going to put me out of my misery anytime soon?"

I swallowed. "Ask again."

Looking me straight in the eyes, Jem licked his lips. "Will you make me the happiest man on earth and marry me, Emily Rose?"

Not sure what came first, the chuckle or the sob. "I will marry you, Jeremy Peter. I will *so* marry you."

The door was flung open all the way and Celia and Marcy jumped in, launching confetti and streamers out of their hand cannons. A colorful shower of paper floated up in the air for a few seconds before falling over everything and everybody. Students yelled in surprise and delight as the rainbow shower covered the room and their heads in bright colored paper.

Jem pulled himself up and drew me into a hug. "Are you crying because you're sad or because you're happy?" he asked me, his mouth by my ear.

Tears were rolling down my face. I probably looked like a deranged raccoon. Pulling myself away from him far enough to look into his oh-so-blue eyes, I giggle-sobbed. "You stupid, stupid fool." I held his face between my hands. "I love you. I have loved you always. Of course they're happy tears. Very happy tears."

"Kiss her, kiss her," the fifth graders were chanting, egged on by my sister and the witch.

Jem took a quick look around us. "Well, I got to tell you," he said in a whisper. "For me it was always you. I love you, Emily Rose."

And he kissed me.

The End

ACKNOWLEDGEMENTS

A special thanks goes to Jenn, fierce leader of our Sippy Cups and Semantics writing group, who shared the wonderful picture that inspired this story. All your pictures inspire me to write. If only I had the time to write all of them.

To my amazing yoga teacher, Aliya, who has helped me find inner peace and a flexibility I didn't know I had. Thank you for all the support and encouragement. And thank you for believing in me.

To all my beta readers, whose enthusiasm for this story made me feel all oozy inside and gave me the pep I needed to keep going. You rock!

To my awesome editors, J.K. and Olivia for doing an amazing job at helping me "clean" and improve my story. Amazing what you don't notice after you read your manuscript a million times.

To my wonderful publisher and master motivator, Becky, for all her support and enthusiasm. It's been a blast!

Since I'm a serious art nerd I have to give kudos to the Hot Tree Publishing graphic team who came up with this amazing cover. Love it!

Last, but never ever least, a huge thank you to my family who put up with my writing growing up and who loved me unconditionally through it all. Love you all.

ABOUT THE AUTHOR

Natalina wrote her first romance in collaboration with her best friend at the age of thirteen. Since then she has ventured into other genres, but romance is first and foremost in almost everything she writes. Her novel, *We Will Always Have the Closet*, is her first published romance.

After earning a degree in tourism and foreign languages, she worked as a tourist guide in her native country, Portugal, for a short time before moving to the United States. She's lived in three continents and a few islands, and her knack for languages and linguistics led her to a master's degree in education. She lives in Virginia where she has taught English as a second language to elementary school children for more years than she cares to admit.

Natalina doesn't believe you can have too many books or too much coffee. Art and dance make her happy and she is pretty sure she could survive on lobster and bananas alone. When she is not writing or stressing over lesson plans, she shares her life with her husband and two adult sons.

Facebook: WWW.FACEBOOK.COM/AUTHORNATALINAREIS

ABOUT THE PUBLISHER

Hot Tree Publishing opened its doors in 2015 with an aspiration to bring quality fiction to the world of readers. With the initial focus on romance and a wide spread of romance sub-genres, we envision opening up to alternative genres in the near future.

Firmly seated in the industry as a leading editing provider to independent authors and small publishing houses, Hot Tree Publishing is the sister company to Hot Tree Editing, founded in 2012. Having established in-house editing and promotions, plus having a well-respected market presence, Hot Tree Publishing endeavors to be a leader in bringing quality stories to the world of readers.

Interested in discovering more amazing reads brought to you by Hot Tree Publishing or perhaps you're interested in submitting a manuscript and joining the HTPubs family? Either way, head over to the website for information:

WWW.HOTTREEPUBLISHING.COM

www.ingramcontent.com/pod-product-compliance
Lightning Source LLC
Chambersburg PA
CBHW050514190726

48284CB00003B/807